ONE DREADFUL NIGHT

ONE DREADFUL NIGHT

Ronald S. L. Harding

With an Introduction by

John Pelan

RAMBLE HOUSE

ISBN 13: 978-1-60543-574-9

ISBN 10: 1-60543-574-0

Cover Art: Gavin L. O'Keefe
Preparation: Fender Tucker

DANCING TUATARA PRESS #19

THE MYSTERIES OF MR. HARDING

The list of British thriller authors from the 1930s includes a number of skilled yet nearly forgotten authors who specialized in treading the ground between the overtly supernatural and those that featured a rationalized explanation of events. Included in this small but illustrious group are Walter S. Masterman, James Corbett, Arlton Eadie, and Ronald S. L. Harding. While both Masterman and Corbett wrote a number of straightforward mysteries, their most intriguing novels are those that kept the reader guessing as to whether or not supernatural forces are actually at work. These novels were paralleled in the U.S. by the "weird menace" magazines typified by *Horror Stories, Terror Tales* and *Dime Mystery Magazine;* where authors such as Arthur J. Burks, Wyatt Blassingame, and John H. Knox were the standard-bearers of the genre. Without a similar venue, the British authors focused on full-length novels as opposed to the novella or novelette prevalent in the U.S.

Splendid examples of this type of yarn include Masterman's *The Green Toad* and *The Curse of Cantire* and Corbett's *Vampire of the Skies.* However, the one author who truly excelled at this type of novel was Ronald S.L. Harding. Little information on Harding is available, and his books are at least as scarce as those of contemporaries such as Mark Hansom and R.R. Ryan.

Whereas the U.S. had the pulp magazines, the market in the U.K. was quite different, with the thriller novels being marketed primarily to the lending libraries. While this strategy generated a wide readership it also accounts for the scarcity of these titles. One of the unfortunate circumstances of this program was the fact that books were literally read to pieces; another factor was the library policy of immediately removing and tossing out the dust jackets of all new arrivals. Some publishers, such as Wright & Brown produced a sturdy if plain product that held up to the multiple readings. Ronald S. L. Harding had the misfortune to be published by London's Modem Publishing Company, an imprint known for both their volume of titles and the shoddiness of their product.

Were these conditions not enough to ensure the survival of only a very few copies of Harding's books an even more devastating circumstance was the bombing of the warehouse district during the blitz. In some cases, entire print runs were destroyed. The author of *Dark Sanctuary,* H.B. Gregory told me that of the 400 copies printed of his classic horror novel the only copies that survived were his personal copies (3) and perhaps a dozen or so copies that had been mailed to reviewers in Canada and Australia.

We have been fortunate enough to secure copies of two of Harding's novels and with luck, we ought to be able to track down at least a couple more of the half-dozen novels known to exist.

One Dreadful Night presents a mystery that is deftly woven into the underlying web of supernatural horror. From the moment that a strange face is glimpsed peering from the window of the laboratory at "Restormal", the novel builds gradually to a climatic resolution of sheer terror as the identity of the mysterious woman lurking in the dim-lit corridors is revealed in a shocking denouement.

One Dreadful Night is part of that small group of novels such as Mark Hansom's *The Beasts of Brahm* wherein the elements of the mystery novel and the supernatural tale are blended seamlessly to create a genuine thriller that will keep the reader turning pages while leaving all the lights on!

Cheers,

John Pelan
Midnight House
Gallup, NM

ONE
DREADFUL
NIGHT

CHAPTER I

"I WANT YOU TO MARRY ME, DORA."

Dora Owen had seen it coming for the past three days or so. In fact during the greater part of her fortnight's stay at "Restormal"—the home of Mr. and Mrs. James Armstrong— she had felt, with that strange intuition peculiar to women, that Robert—the son of the house—took quite an exceptional interest in his mother's young guest.

And when we say "an exceptional interest" what we mean is that it was very exceptional indeed for Robert Armstrong to take *any* interest whatever in a member of the weaker sex, for he was no ordinary young man—far from it.

Just over thirty years of age, he was, both in manner and appearance, seemingly very much older; a quiet, self-contained, thoughtful-looking scientist, who spent the greater part of his life in his laboratory, poring over ancient books and mysterious instruments and apparatus—apparently alive to nothing else save these tools of his learned trade.

Young as he was, he had, already, begun to make his name famous in the scientific world in which he seemed quite absorbed, and, more than once, it had been said of him that he would cause all living men of science to be forgotten; that he would stand out alone as the greatest electrochemical investigator of his generation.

No slight praise, either, in this age of scientific genius.

As may be imagined, he was anything but a gallant, gay Lothario in looks. A tall, thin, bespectacled figure, he lived in a land of dreams about bones, bottles, electro-magnets, and Leyden jars; to say nothing of butterflies, moths, beetles, and snails, of which, by the way, he had an enormous collection all pinned or glued into showcases with which his bedroom was lined.

He only slept when absolutely necessary, and, had it not been for the compulsion of a maternal government, he would, in all probability, have starved to death through sheer absent-mindedness. Even when dragged to the family table by main force, he handled his knife and fork as though he were dissecting his meat, and cutting his potatoes into micro-slide sections. And as to his green vegetables—well, on one great occasion, a careless cook boiled some unfortunate grub in the runner beans, and, as luck would have it, this choice morsel found its way on to Robert's plate—

"And the absent-minded Robert ate it—how horrible!" did you say?

Not a bit of it, dear reader. That is just what he did *not* do—he *saw* it!

Now most young men dislike finding maggots in their beans; but not so Robert. He loved it. You see, it appeared that this particular creature—although a mere horrid grub to Tom, Dick, and Harry—was something quite different to the learned Robert.

Whether it had come out of Tutankh-Amen's tomb origi-nally, and had, in some mysterious way, got into the beans; or was the missing link between grub and vegetable, we will not, in our miserable ignorance, pretend to say: anyway, it was a singularly rare and valuable kind of grub—just the sort Robert had hunted for in vain since early childhood, and so, madly delighted, he picked it carefully out of the surround-ing scarlet-runners, and, with a shout of triumph, dashed up-stairs to his laboratory, where he remained for the nest twenty-four hours or so, making a microscopical and electro-chemical examination of his prize, muttering, the while, pro-found Greek and Latin terms under his bated breath.

Ultimately, we believe, he had it stuffed! In the meantime, however, he dispatched a lengthy article to a scientific jour-nal, and, during the following week, a miniature army of white-haired and grey-bearded old men besieged the place, all passionately eager to inspect the find, and, when accorded this happiness, all holding different opinions as to exactly what it was, and how in the name of wonder it had got into the beans—opinions which quickly developed into heated arguments, and, finally—it is said (we won't vouch for the truth of the statement) led to an extraordinary general meeting of the Royal Society.

Which all goes to show that Robert Armstrong was not exactly the kind of young man a girl could flirt with. Still, as few, if any, girls ever tried, no one was inconvenienced.

When Dora Owen was introduced to him upon her arrival at "Restormal," her first impression had been that he was a singularly disagreeable young fellow with detestable manners and certainly not worth the trouble of a second thought. It was not long, however, before she noticed that this opinion was not reciprocated, for Robert soon began to develop certain symptoms.

For one thing he started to appear regularly at meals: for another, it was observed that his tie, instead of reposing under his left ear, suddenly assumed its proper position: again, that, whereas, normally, he not infrequently wore odd shoes —one black and one brown, for instance—now his right foot invariably matched his left in every particular: and, finally, that his hair—which as a rule stood on end "like quills upon the fretful porcupine"—now looked comparatively tidy.

Then, one summer evening, instead of creeping about the garden with a dark lantern, a butterfly net, and a tin box, as was his wont, he was seen to cut flowers—not those weird, wild little things botanists love to press, but real, cultivated garden flowers—big, sweet-scented, red and white roses— break the thorns off the stalks, and, actually, present them to Dora—and then bolt as if he had committed a "smash and grab" robbery.

Next he started to write her little notes asking her to go out with him, which at first she studiously ignored in spite of having to read them under his very nose at the breakfast table, perhaps just because of it. "How ridiculous to post a letter to a person in the same house!" she thought to herself on these occasions. But, in spite of the way she scorned them, these little notes still continued to come. And then, when she stole a glance at him over the table—just to see how he was taking his punishment—and caught him looking at her with big, pathetic, unhappy eyes, she turned away quickly because she felt herself flushing all over for no reason whatever.

"Oh, well—perhaps he isn't so bad, after all," she thought, later on to herself, and began to realise that the reason he wrote to her instead of speaking was simply that he was quite tongue-tied in her presence.

So one day she buttonholed him after receiving a more than usually urgent epistle, and accepted the invitation it contained—with the result that, a few evenings later, she accompanied him to a theatre—an outing which became the first of many.

Gradually his excessive shyness wore off; bit by bit his frozen tongue got into working order; and evenings which they did not spend at theatres or dances—at which functions, by the way, Robert actually wore some approach to evening-dress; a proceeding filling everyone with stark, staring, amazement—were spent strolling together in the lovely old-world garden at "Restormal."

During these strolls, Dora discovered her admirer to have a surprisingly poetic mentality for such a formidable man of science; and that while he was able to tell her some quite interesting facts about the purely botanical side of the beautiful flowers they were among, he both could and did say other things about them: things which thrilled her too.

And, ultimately, matters came to a head when, one glorious moonlight night in September, he asked her point-blank to marry him, and in the very words with which this chapter opens.

Now, although she had almost daily expected that something like this would happen, Dora really did not know quite what to say. So to gain time, she started to pull the petals off the rose in her dress, and to throw them one by one on to the garden path.

After about the tenth had fluttered to the ground, Robert repeated his words, a trifle more urgently, and gradually slipped an arm round her unresisting waist.

"I want you to marry me, Dora!"

By this time the petals were all gone—even the stalk had been torn up into tiny bits and dropped on to the bed of pink leaves at her feet.

But still Dora had not quite settled in her mind how to answer him.

So she just murmured one word—

"Why?"

"Because I want you never to leave me," he replied. "I couldn't bear it—I don't know what I should do without you!"

"But you've only known me a fortnight!"

"It's been the only happy fortnight of my life."

"But hasn't all the rest of your life been happy?"

"In a sense, yes: that's to say, I've been buried in my work, and alive to nothing else. But, although I did not know it, I was suffering all the time from want of you. My work has been nothing more than a kind of anesthetic which has prevented me from realising my own unhappiness—nothing more. And now—now that I have seen in you the living embodiment of half-forgotten dreams—I have awakened to the fullest sense of my bitter need. Having once known happiness, how can I go back again to the old life in which it had no part? If you leave here it can only mean that I shall have to drag out an existence of a terrible loneliness I can't bear even to think of."

"Do I really mean such a lot to you then?"

"Can you ask?"

"But I never dreamed it possible, Robert, really, I never thought for one instant that you were the kind of man who would ever look twice at any woman."

"But you know differently now?"

"Yes," she whispered.

"And you know that I love you?"

"Yes."

"And you love me?"

"I don't know what to say."

"Say yes."

"Yes."

"And so you will marry me?"

"If you really want me so badly, I suppose I'd better."

Almost at the same instant as Dora uttered these words, a beetle was observed to be climbing cautiously up the front of her dress. No doubt it had dropped there from the roses which grew so thickly round the rustic archway under which they stood. She caught sight of it. and, having a rooted aversion to creepy things of every description, gave vent to a little scream of terror.

"Oh, look . . . look . . ."

Now this particular beetle was an amazingly long legged beetle, and, in the ordinary way, would have been a great find for a young man of Robert Armstrong's tastes. But, somehow, he didn't think of it quite like this just now, and, instead of carefully transferring the remarkable specimen to the little bottle he always carried in one of his pockets for the accommodation of scientific treasures like this, he seemed to regard it in something the same light as St. George did the dragon. Anyway, he hastened forthwith to the rescue of his lady from the monster which assailed her, and hurling it to the ground with a very unlearned violence, would have actually trodden it underfoot in savage fury for daring to sully the dainty beauty of her sacred dress, and frighten her so with its ugly waving antennae, but for the fact that the beetle—having been trained from infancy to avoid human boots—skillfully evaded his angry stamp and scuttled hurriedly away to its family: feeling, no doubt, very thankful to have escaped a felon's death, and, naturally enough, leaving the couple it had disturbed locked tightly in each other's arms, where they remained—quite oblivious of anything or anybody—for the next hour or so.

Dora had done it. She had become engaged to this odd-looking scientist, and, strange to say, she felt rather pleased about it than otherwise—although if, a fortnight, nay, even a week, ago, someone had told her that this would come about, she would have been very indignant indeed, and, doubtless, declared that she "positively *hated* him!"

Now when a woman "positively hates" a man, all wise friends start saving up their pennies to buy wedding presents, for the simple reason that this kind of hatred nearly always shows that an exceptional interest has been aroused—also that the hated one has failed to do something which in the opinion—very secret opinion though—of the hater, he should: and which, as a rule, is to "pop the Question"—of course only to give her the pleasure of refusing him (?)

And, really, things had been very much like this in the present instance. Dora had been tremendously interested in Robert Armstrong right from the very first—in her heart of hearts—and only formed her first opinion that he was a "most disagreeable young man" because he had not been over-cordial to her upon being formally introduced. "Hell hath no fury like a woman scorned," of course, and she had looked upon this as tantamount to scorn, and so set out to break down his reserve: finally, as we have seen, falling herself into the pit she had dug for her neighbour, by becoming insanely in love with him—a state of affairs, by the way, she never quite recognised until he had plucked up courage enough to put his arms round her. And this did it. She suddenly realised that she despised all ordinary young men; that she had caught one in a thousand; that, really, he was an Adonis—underneath those spectacles—although she was the only one who knew it—no other girl would be intelligent enough to appreciate a human marvel like Robert. And so forth.

Besides, as to his weird appearance, it had its advantages. You see, there never was a woman yet who did not believe, in the bottom of her soul, that every other woman thought of nothing else, night and day, but how to get hold of *her* particular man, and take him away from her, and Dora regarded her lover's oddness as a kind of veil behind which his manly beauty could be hidden from the prying eyes of bold bad women, who, otherwise, would want him themselves, and so lead him astray to her personal loss. She felt, in fact, that it was a kind of insurance against the dangers to which women possessing normal men were exposed, and would not have changed him for worlds.

Truly, she knew very little about him, since she had only known him a fortnight: but then Dora prided herself upon being a pretty sound judge of character, and Robert—in so far as he could be gauged by ordinary standards—gave her no reason to doubt that he was in every respect an estimable enough young fellow with a gentle, kindly nature, and no vices in particular—except his work: while to crown every-thing—he had ample private means. And this—as we all know—will cover a multitude of sins: the universal ten-dency, in cultivated society, being to look upon most com-fortably-off young men as sound and reliable people—and to regard all poor and struggling ones as scoundrels and adven-turers. Not that Dora was in the least mercenary—or even one of those women who regard marriage as a kind of com-mercial proposition requiring a banker's reference or its equivalent—the idea of getting anything out of their relation-ship never occurred to her, and, had he been utterly penni-less, it would have made not the least difference. She had met him, and loved him; and determined, therefore, that, since he wanted her, she must become—not his principal creditor from the perpetual presentation of whose bill there could be no escape day or night (i.e. about the worst type of lady of the street corner known)—but the one person in the world whose devotion was entirely independent of whatever fate or fortune might hold for its object, and remain a faithful helper until death: the haven in storm, and the light in dark-ness. Dora felt, instinctively, that Robert badly needed the tender care of a devoted woman, and determined that, at all costs, he should have it, rejoicing in his financial stability only because it would make it all the more easy for her to minister to his purely physical comfort.

Thus Robert was singularly fortunate in his choice of a wife: the more so as, in addition to her womanly sweetness of disposition, Dora was, beyond question, some-thing well worthwhile possessing from the purely physical standpoint—

a lovely vision which once seen by any man was calculated to linger long and sweetly in his memory.

And girls of this description are not picked up every day in the week to say the least of it.

For some time the lovers remained clasped together under the starlit heaven, lip to lip, and breast to breast: mute with the fond rapture of their golden hour. Robert only ceased to kiss the soft lips, which, so miraculously, it seemed, had become his own, when quite breathless with exhaustion, gazing the while into the tender depth of the dear eyes which looked so lovingly into his own.

"I love you, I love you!" he murmured.

Dora drew one dimpled arm from around his shoulders, and smoothed his hair gently with her hand.

"It's very late, dearest," she whispered, "we ought to go in."

"Not yet," he begged, "not yet. I can hardly believe that I'm awake: often, so often, I have held you like this in my dreams, only to wake to nothingness again, and, almost, I fear to be separated from you even for an instant, in case I find that I have opened my eyes once more to be unloved and alone."

She wrapped him again in her arms, and, as she did so, her dark hair, which she wore long in frank defiance of fashion, came tumbling over her shoulders, and he buried his face in its thick silken tresses.

"Marry me soon," he breathed into her ear.

"Of course, darling—as soon as possible," she answered, "but don't you think that, possibly, this is really the happiest time?"

"It is indeed," replied her lover, "but because I hold you in my arms, and know that you are mine: and I want you to marry me quickly that this may continue for ever and a day: that we may never have to part again: that no power, save death, may take you from me."

He led her to one of the rustic seats which flanked the interior of the rose-covered archway, and, sitting down without letting her go—as if fearful that she might slip away from him—gathered her to his heart.

And then—just as they sat there, bathed in the silver moonlight: two human beings twined so closely in each other's embrace as to appear one, the silence of the perfect night in which, up to now, only the muted sighing of the faint breeze in the treetops could be heard, was broken by the softest of trills: a sound which seemed to rise from the ground somewhere in the distance, and swell out like a crescendo of sweet music—ever ascending and ascending higher and higher into the star-spangled heavens.

"Do you hear it?" whispered Dora, and her lover nodded.

It was the last Nightingale of Summer, singing his tenderest song as if for a parting benediction to the lovers before he left for the blue-skyed Mediterranean—filling the garden with its inexpressible beauty, and the hearts of his listeners with thoughts which were indeed "beyond the reaching of their souls"—perhaps half-voicing an unuttered prayer that time might cease to pass in that moment of perfect happiness.

Little as Dora and Robert wanted to break the spell and leave that moonlit garden, they felt, at last, compelled to come down more or less to earth;—and, realising that it must be well past one in the morning, and that, if they stayed out much longer, they ran a risk of having their sweet privacy disturbed by somebody coming out to look for them,—they slowly walked back to the house together with their arms about one another, along the flower-bordered, crazy-flagged path, which led them from their rose covered archway between the tennis and croquet lawns to the verandah at the back of "Restormal" from which a glass door would admit them to the drawing-room.

Walking slowly through the sultry air which was so heavily laden with the scent of many flowers, more than half lost in dreams, and hardly looking where they were going, the loving pair had traversed about three-quarters of the hundred yards to the house, when, suddenly, Dora seemed to sense something, looked up, and gripped Robert's arm with a little gasp of half-suppressed terror.

"Oh look . . . look!" she gasped.

"What is it?" said Robert sharply, and there was something in his voice which suggested that he was gripped by a nearly forgotten fear—that he all but dreaded what she might reply.

"Tell me dear, for Heaven's sake—what is it?"

"Your laboratory window, Robert,—look!"

"Restormal" was a solid, square, many storied mansion, thickly covered with ivy and creeper, and loomed up in the silver light of the moon like some great ghost-castle, throwing a gigantic shadow across the gleaming white lawn which sloped down to the flower-garden they had just left. Robert's laboratory was an enormous room at the very top of the house, lighted in front by a skylight, and, at the back, by a dormer window which jutted out of the tiles. In company with a couple of unused attics, and much loft-space, it formed the whole of a storey approached by a narrow winding stairway leading from another little-used floor, and had been selected by Robert for the scene of his labours on account of its quietness and seclusion from the disturbing influences of the domestic life below. It was, of course, a sacred spot in the household, and seldom, if ever, visited by anyone save Robert himself: so one might well expect that at one in the morning—when its owner was standing below in the garden—it would be in absolute darkness, and quite uninhabited.

But to-night that little window peeping out from beneath the eaves, gleamed out into the darkness with a dim, greenish light, which flickered as though it came from a corpse-candle;—and pressed against the curtainless panes, looking down into the garden, and wearing a dreadful expression of inveterate hatred, was a withered, yellow face.

CHAPTER II

DORA SHRUNK CLOSE AGAINST HER LOVER.

"Who is it?" she whispered, "who is it?"

For quite ten seconds he made no reply, and, in the tense silence, Dora thought that she could hear his teeth chattering. Then, suddenly, the face at the window disappeared, and with it that eerie, phosphorescent light. At the same instant as it did so, Robert drew a deep breath, pulled himself together with an effort, and said,—

"What is it dear?—who's—"

"Surely you saw it, Robert," she broke in, still trembling, though thankful that the dreadful apparition had gone, "that face . . . that yellow, withered face at your laboratory window."

He forced a laugh.

"You must be dreaming, sweetheart—there's no face at that window up there."

"It's gone now, Robert: but if I stand here I saw it, and not two minutes ago either—staring down here as if it were looking at us. Its expression was terrible . . . and it had hair too, long, white hair; and a horrible claw of a hand . . . Robert . . . what was it . . . you must have seen it too . . . surely you must . . . ."

"You forget, dear, that I am very shortsighted," he made answer, "but I'm pretty sure that there is nobody up in my laboratory:"

"But I *know* there is . . . I *saw* . . . *It* . . . *!* "

"You saw what?"

"That face—Oh, what could it have been?"

"It must have been one of the servants, dearest: wonder what she was doing up there," he replied. But his voice lacked conviction, and Dora could see, even in the pale moonlight, that he was deathly white, while beads of perspiration stood out on his brow.

Dora had seen every member of the household staff; but not one of them, she knew, even faintly resembled that mask-like face: in fact she had never before dreamed that any human being could look quite like that. It had looked like a living corpse.

"I'm sure it wasn't any of the servants," she said, "it couldn't have been . . ."

"Perhaps it was the skull of one of my skeletons then," said Robert; "anyhow, dearest, I'll go up and see just what it was."

They were in the house by now, and Dora was able to see, in the glare of the electric light, that Robert was gripping the lapels of his coat with both hands, and that his fingers were twitching convulsively.

"What's the matter, Robert?" she asked gently. "You look terrible?"

"Nothing," he replied, "nothing at all," and she noticed that he could not look her in the eyes. "Just a little cold— that's all darling: you'd better go up to bed, and I'll see if there is anyone up in my laboratory . . . I'm sure that there is not."

Dora was about to speak when Robert's mother entered the room.

Mrs. James Armstrong was a white-haired, tallish woman of sixty, with a sibilant sweetness of manner which more often than not suggested, if not actual insincerity, at least something very like it. She floated across to where Robert and Dora were standing—just inside the French windows— slipped the bolt, and drew across the heavy curtains, saying, as she did so:

"Isn't it time you children went up to bed—do you know it's past one?"

Then suddenly she noticed their white, strained faces.

"Why what's the matter, dears—you both look like ghosts?"

Robert Armstrong looked at his mother steadily for the fraction of a second and replied:

"Dora's had rather a scare, mother,—she thinks she's seen a face up in the laboratory . . ."

Just for an instant Dora imagined that something like fear flashed into Mrs. Armstrong's eyes: the next moment the impression was gone.

"You must have been imagining things, Dora dear," she smiled. "The laboratory is quite empty—nobody ever goes up there but Robert himself—it's the effect of late hours."

"But there was a light, a green flickering light—and I saw a face distinctly," insisted Dora.

Mrs. Armstrong turned to her son,

"Did you see this bogey, Robert?" she asked.

"No, mother," he replied, "but I could hardly have seen a face up there from the garden in any case so—"

"Of course, dear boy—your poor eyes. Still, I can't help thinking Dora must have been dreaming."

Dora shuddered. "I only wish I felt so sure," she said.

"Well, Robert will go up there and look if you like," rejoined Mrs. Armstrong, yawning slightly. "If anybody's been there he'll know: I always say that he keeps count of every speck of dust up in that place."

But Dora clung frantically to her lover.

"Don't go," she implored, "don't leave me . . . I'm frightened."

Neither Robert nor his mother pressed the point. Mrs. Armstrong, however, was all concern at Dora's terror.

"Poor dear child," she said, "you're trembling all over: you mustn't let your imagination run away with you like this you know—come along, dear, to the dining-room and have a glass of wine before you go to bed: a good night's rest will make S*uch* a difference—you'll laugh at it all to-morrow, won't she, Robert?"

"Of course," he answered—but there was something strange in his tone.

"That's right," said his mother cheerfully. "And now how about telling me what kept you two in the garden all the evening—you must have been there nearly four hours: I'm sure you've both got a wonderful secret—surely you did more all that time than see bogey faces in windows which were not there: why, I declare, Dora's blushing already."

Dora suddenly remembered that her hair was hanging loose round her shoulders, and flushed up to the eyes in confusion under her prospective mother-in-law's scrutiny.

"Come on, chickens—out with it," continued that worthy."

So they told her of the relationship which had grown up between them during the past fourteen days and had suddenly burst into full bloom this starlight September evening. She kissed first Dora and then Robert very fondly, and really seemed heartily pleased at the tidings.

"I'm delighted, my dear," she said to Dora: "you know I almost hoped that something of this sort would happen: it's time Robert had a humanising influence in his life: he's always been so very odd. I must say he's shown very excellent taste too. It's something to find a girl who remembers that a woman's hair is her glory, and who has not forgotten how to blush in these painfully modern days. Bless you both! May you have every happiness!"

She kissed them once more, and led the way to the dining-room.

In spite of every assurance, both from her lover and from Mrs. Armstrong, that the dreadful apparition she had seen was no more than a figment of imagination, Dora felt far too frightened to be alone that night, and so it was arranged that she should share a bedroom with Robert's sister, Kathleen, who laughed so long and heartily at the very idea of a horrible presence in her brother's laboratory that, in spite of herself, Dora felt a trifle reassured.

The sight *does* play one funny tricks sometimes!

Kathleen was twenty, and in every respect the reverse of her brother. It would have been difficult indeed to find another pair of relatives so thoroughly dissimilar. Plump and shortish in build, with frizzy blonde hair and merry blue eyes full of mischief, she was a thorough-going modern, spending much of her time, and still more of "poor old pop's" money, in London's dance halls, and other places of the lighter and more expensive kinds of popular entertainment, whither she was often conducted, and still more often escorted back home again, by flaxen-haired youths of the "very nace" and "absolutely topping" variety; who after hanging round her ample person for a few days—or a few weeks, as the case might be—disappeared as mysteriously and inconsequently as they had come. These gentlemen of limited vocabulary and still more limited intellect were, upon occasion, varied by young bloods of the motor-bicycle and wireless-set type, who sported flannel trousers and sweaters, had their pockets full of oil-cans and screwdrivers, and their heads always un-adorned by either hat or cap: possibly as a kind of set off against the dinner-jackets and speckled plus-fours of their deadly rivals, who, not infrequently owned—that's to say had paid the first installment upon—aluminium racing cars as long, thin, light, and fast as they were themselves.

But Kathleen cared for none of them. She thought much more about such things as tennis, croquet, swimming, and dog-racing varied by an occasional flutter on the Derby, than she did of any callow youth be he never so amorous—and, listening far more intently for the dinner gong than she did for the honk of the horn of even the most expensive car of the most lovelorn swain, plied her knife and fork with such heart-whole good will that—like Grimm's sausage—she shone with salt and fat.

What a jolly girl to be sure—just the kind to scare away the horrors.

And scare them away she did most effectively: for Dora, instead of lying awake all night trembling as she would have done had she been in her own room alone with her terror, slept the sleep of the just—although rejecting Kathleen's of-fer of a share in a surreptitious pork pie.

Dating back to early Tudor times, "Restormal" stood in about two and a half acres of ground, some fifteen miles from London. Although upon purchasing the freehold some twenty years before this story opened, its owner, Mr. James Armstrong, had spent a very considerable sum upon its reconditioning, and had it brought thoroughly up-to-date, it still retained much of that venerable gloom so characteristic of ancient houses—especially since the decorators had been careful not to destroy its old-world atmosphere, and Mr. Armstrong had a collection of antique furniture which was generally reckoned as second to none. Also, by way of contrast, he had an array of ultra-modern domestic electrical equipment which would have put any ideal home exhibition to shame, and which,—together with its fruit-flooded orchard and really beautiful flower-garden, tennis courts, and croquet lawns,—made "Restormal" the most desirable of homes.

At the period in which this story opens Mr. James Armstrong was about sixty-five years of age, and spent most of his time either gathering material in London for a "Magnum Opus" of his upon the industrial applications of electricity, or collating that material in his library. He did not concern himself in the least about the affairs of the household, which he left entirely to his wife, who, in turn—not having any great interest in things domestic—left it all to the small staff of servants, who, of course, did exactly as they liked (i.e. as far as possible nothing at all)—did it very well too!

Mary, the cook, and chief of staff, having a comparatively high sense of duty, saw to it that tolerably eatable meals appeared with reasonable regularity—although she had an unfortunate habit of over-ordering from the tradesmen, and consequently putting away "bits," and then forgetting exactly where she had put them. Being, as a rule, of a perishable nature, and sometimes of considerable size—a six-pound joint of meat or a couple of dozen herrings for instance—these "bits" generally automatically made known their hiding-place, and, sooner or later—but mostly later—were discovered either converted by nature into edible cradles for infant bluebottles, or adorned with purple fungi—and, in every case, in a distinctly "nifty" condition.

It being thought that this little failing on the part of the otherwise estimable Mary was due, possibly, to overwork, a bright young thing of nineteen was called in to assist her in her labours. This bright young thing, we regret to relate, had, ultimately, to be suppressed on account of her presenting the butcher's boy with twins, and his subsequent refusal to lead her to the altar on the grounds that at least one of them belonged to the milkman—or rather that it was not the milkman's fault if it didn't.

In spite of the repeated assurances on the part of the happy mother to the effect that the birth of her twins was miraculous, the stern morality of Mary the cook suffered a severe shock from her assistant's lapse. After the unlucky event had blown over and she reigned once more in solitary state over the affairs of the kitchen—merely calling in such non-residential assistance from outside as she found necessary—her memory, which was never exactly her strong point, gave way almost entirely. Either she forgot to take the meat out of the oven until it had been reduced to a smoky cinder, or she was so anxious to avoid such overroasting that she omitted, in her confusion of mind, to put the oven on at all. Further, she mislaid not only twice as many "bits" as before, but everything else she touched, declaring with the most solemn oaths when asked for the key of the safe that she had never laid a finger on it, while, all the time, it reposed in her "pocket"—a canvas affair dangling from a waistband under her skirt—from which, eventually, it would be produced, generally improved by contact with the remains of eggs or tomatoes which also had been deposited in that bag of mystery and come to grief.

Another unfortunate weakness of hers—and one which she could be well excused since it was shared by every other member of the household save Mr. James Armstrong himself who didn't count except when the bills came in—was, that, unaccustomed to using electric light, which she would insist upon calling "the gas," she could only call to mind one use of a switch—that was the putting of a light or an oven *on*. Hence, every light she used was *never* off either by day or by

night except on those not infrequent occasions when the fuse
blew or a lamp was smashed. It is quite true that she only
had access to a comparatively restricted area, but then Kathleen, Robert, and Mrs. Armstrong never could remember to
put out "the gas" either, so there really was very little darkness anywhere or anytime.

Now "Restormal" had some nineteen or twenty rooms,
twelve large cupboards, and four good-sized cellars, to say
nothing of its numerous passageways, corridors, and stair-
cases, all fitted with nice, bright, extravagant, half-watt
lamps, and, in some instances, bowl fires as well. So it was
not altogether surprising that the little indicators on the electric light and power meters worked perpetual overtime.
Morn, noon, and night, they went round, and round, and
round, like tiny windmills in a super hurricane, with the
gratifying result that every quarter Mr. James Armstrong received a bill for electricity which would have been excessive
if he had run a chain of factories. In fact, the supply company imagined that he must certainly carry on some exceptionally expensive form of manufacture, and not only
charged him at a special rate per unit—the privilege of only
the very heaviest consumers—but presented him with a box
of cigars every Christmas as their best customer.

Now one would have thought that Mr. Armstrong would
have been very grateful to his valuable servant for having
obtained him such unusual concessions. But it was apparently not so, because every time one of the temporary skiv-
vys discovered a burned out oven—or some gadget or other
exploded from being left on for five weeks on end—and informed Mary of the fact, she invariably would mutter
"Shush!—if Mr. Armstrong knew that—he'd go mad!"

But, in spite of every attempt to spare him, know it he did
sooner or later, and "went mad" with a right good will every
quarter day, calling Mary—together with every other member of the household—into the library, and expounding at
great length upon the value of economy, and the costliness of
waste, imploring them all with tears in his eyes to put off

"the gas" at least occasionally—anyhow during the hours of daylight.

But the only effect his orations ever had was to create a hazy sort of impression in Mary's not over-powerful mind that in some mysterious way her employer was losing money, and that something must be done to save him from speedy ruin. So, after one of these interviews, she would beseech local tradesmen to "let her have things cheap" to save "poor Mr. Armstrong's pocket," and hint darkly to all and sundry that he was fast going dead broke. But the lights blazed merrily away twenty-four hours a day just the same as before, and the good soul's efforts had no result other than to create a rumour for miles around that Mr. Armstrong was ruined—whereat the shopkeepers one and all got a panic and started sending in their bills.

Now although Mr. Armstrong certainly *was* losing money regularly every quarter day to the local electric light company—and to a good few other commercial undertakings too,—it was rather overstating the case to say that he was rapidly becoming financially unstable, so poor Mary the cook found herself in hot water once again without being able to realise quite why.

Even when she woke up the gardener—who had a pleasant little way of sitting on his wheelbarrow and going to sleep all day long (except, of course, at meal times), courageously leaving his work to two boy assistants who never did a stroke unless they were watched—and confided the matter to his alert mind, all he could do was to scratch his head and say,—

"Eee, Mary, ye must ha' done somethin'!" and then doze off to sleep again, leaving Mary still wondering what she could have done—quite unable to see that she had got into trouble quite as much for leaving undone those things she ought to have done as for doing that which she ought not.

Now as the worthies mentioned above comprised the entire resident domestic staff at "Restormal" with the exception of one odd job boy who perpetually applied the principles of practical communism to his master's property without ever

being found out save by the gardener's boy who demanded a
share in exchange for silence and got it—it will not, perhaps,
altogether surprise the reader to learn that things domestic in
the Armstrong household did not always run as smoothly or
as economically as they might.

But since Mr. Armstrong himself was too busy to make
many enquiries and too wealthy to be forced to: Robert was
buried in his studies and experiments: Kathleen entirely pre-
occupied in warding off young men and taking nourishment:
and Mrs. Armstrong took no interest, perhaps it didn't really
matter much, after all.

Still, there are limits to everything, and above all to the un-
necessary expenditure of money: and so, as each succeeding
quarter day brought in its amazingly inflated bills, Mr. Armstrong became progressively more and more angry. But his
ire was especially aroused by the accounts he received from
the Electric Power Supply Company: because, you see, electricity was his subject, and so he was enabled to see very
clearly that there was actual waste in this direction—whereas
in the case of ordinary household accounts he left the check-
ing up to be done by his wife who always "O.K.'d" every
and any bill without looking at it.

Now although the actual responsibility for the waste of
electricity at "Restormal" was pretty equally divided between all parties concerned—viz:—Mrs. Armstrong, Robert,
Kathleen, and the kitchen staff—yet, somehow, they managed to shift the whole of the blame upon the shoulders of
Mary the cook—who, having no memory to speak of, and
being a mere hireling to boot, was, of course, most admirably
adapted for the purpose—especially as she really did no
more than her share.

Mary was exceedingly fond of her employers—especially
of Mr. Armstrong himself for whom she would cheerfully
have died—and so it was a source of the deepest grief to her
to find herself brought continually to book for having left on
"the gas" at all times and in all places. She worried herself to
death over it: and, naturally enough, the more she worried

the more fuddled became her poor brain and the more often she offended. Try as she might she could not keep out of trouble: and it preyed upon her mind so much that, not infrequently, it kept her awake at night.

So although Dora slept the sleep of the just to the accompaniment of a non-stop snore from Kathleen—who was, doubtless, dreaming that the whole world had become one vast suet pudding and that she had the eating of it—all but convinced in her mind that the yellow face she had seen at Robert's laboratory window had been nothing more than a figment of imagination, there were others in the household who did not—notably Mary the cook.

She had seen no yellow face truly—but an even worse bogey stood between her and her slumbers: and that resolved itself into such awful questions as:—had she left the light on anywhere? was that oven still running? etc.

The poor soul could not for the life of her remember—in fact it was nearly four in the morning before she was even able to call to mind exactly what she was worrying about. She thought, and thought, and thought, and racked her head until it would have ached had it contained anything capable of aching—had she left on "the gas"?

At last she determined to go down and see for herself.

She slipped out of bed, put on a dressing gown and slippers, and stole downstairs. Here she had a bit of a shock.

Every light in the house appeared to be on—and she knew perfectly well that even if she had not left them on herself she would certainly get the blame if they should be discovered. Mr. Armstrong was away for a few days truly, but then he'd be sure to hear of it the moment he returned, and Mary trembled in her check felt slippers.

There was nothing for it but to make a complete tour of the ground floor, and she accordingly made that tour, putting out lights and electric fires by the score en route.

Finally she had only the dining-room to inspect. But, when she put her hand on the door knob, she was amazed to hear voices from inside.

Somebody was still up. Who could it be? Heavens! Suppose the master of the house had come home before his time and found all those lights!

Now, as one of Mary's many weaknesses was an intense curiosity as to the sayings and doings of those around her because she always firmly believed that all and sundry ran her down behind her back, we deeply regret to relate that she listened outside the door.

But the voices were so muffled that all she was able to learn in full five minutes was that one of the speakers was a man and the other a woman.

Who could they be? They were talking in low, hushed voices: and there was something in the tone of those inaudible mutterings which gave her the creeps—especially as now and again she fancied she caught the words "poor boy," "dreadful," "destroy," and, finally, "death."

Suddenly she heard the key turn from within, and she shrank away immediately behind a pair of heavy plush curtains. Directly opposite the dining-room door, these veiled the entry to the lounge, and enabled her to watch without very much risk of being seen, although her heart was beating so loudly that she dreaded lest it should be heard in that deathly silence.

The dining-room door opened slowly. Robert and his mother came out of the room, and Mary noticed that Mrs. Armstrong's eyes were swollen as if she had been crying for hours, and that Robert's face was deathly white and set hard. Together they crept upstairs as if they were retiring to rest, disappearing round the bend of the broad oak staircase.

They had not seen her, and, thankful to have escaped notice. Mary, after waiting until sufficient time had elapsed to allow them to get to their respective rooms, slipped shivering from her hiding-place and ran upstairs to bed again, falling to sleep the moment her head touched the pillow although not without wondering drowsily exactly what it all meant.

Perhaps neither Mary nor Dora, nor even the happy-go-lucky Kathleen, would have had much sleep that night if they could have known that Robert and Mrs. Armstrong, instead of going to their rooms after that secret midnight confab, had crept step by step, inch by inch, slowly up flight after flight of deserted stairway, right up to that eerie top floor of the old house which was occupied solely by two empty attics—and Robert's chemical laboratory.

Both of them were trembling from head to foot, and their faces ashen-grey with a terrible fear—while in his hand Robert carried a heavy revolver.

CHAPTER III

IT IS AN EXTRAORDINARY FACT that the lower the standard of a person's intellect, the less able is that person to abstain from talking. Now as talking has been defined as the audible expression of ideas, one would surely imagine that a great amount of it must needs imply a correspondingly high birthrate of thought. But the funny part of it is that, in actual practice, one nearly always finds that the conversation of the perpetual chatterer is—to put it mildly—of a distinctly C 3 variety. In fact, the non-stop cackler generally has one idea, and one only, which is that every living soul is simply dying to be regaled with his—or more usually her—views on the deeds and misdeeds—but especially the misdeeds—of other people.

Such a one was Mary the cook. She could no more have kept anything to herself than she could have translated St. Mark's Gospel from the Greek: and the odd part of it was that whereas she was quite incapable of remembering such trifles as having left a light on or where she had put down anything five seconds ago, or for the matter of that anything else whatever, yet she *never* forgot any single detail capable of being converted into gossip, any more than she ever failed to hold forth at great length on every possible occasion.

Not only so, but on these occasions she actually exhibited inventive genius by way of re-arranging and embellishing the truth to such a degree that she invariably set the entire neighbourhood by the ears on an average of three times a week, often without a single fact to help her.

It will not surprise the reader, therefore, to learn that when Mary the cook awoke the morning after she had witnessed the tail end of the midnight confab between Robert and his mother, it was not long before she took every willing member of the household into her confidence, including, of course, the milkman, the grocer, the butcher, the baker, the fishmonger, and the greengrocer—or rather their respective "boys"—when they called for orders: to say nothing of the dustman and the chimneysweep in person.

Mary held these gentry in the highest esteem, addressed them one and all as "lovey," and had the deepest confidence in their opinions upon any and every subject. So much so that if an utterance on the part of any one of them disagreed with the view on the same matter expressed, say, in *The Times*—well, *The Times* was wrong, that's all—at least as far as Mary the cook was concerned.

So she submitted the present mystery of the midnight meeting between mother and son, and the strange words she had heard from behind the locked door, to the infallible judgment of each individually, as, one by one, they rang the tradesmen's bell—together with the news that "Master Robert" had engaged himself to Dora Owen.

"Coo," said the baker's boy scornfully, scratching his head with the corner of a tin loaf as he lounged against the lintel of the door, "there ain't no mystery about this—can't yer see?"

Mary couldn't, and the baker's boy—after dropping the loaf into the mud in his excitement, wiping it on the seat of his trousers, and burying it under the others in his basket to palm off on to another client by the simple method of leaving it on the step because he "couldn't wait"—waxed eloquent.

"Well now—see 'ere," said he. " 'Er son, wot is the apple of 'er eye, goes and gits mixed up with this girl wot's stayin' 'ere, and tells 'is mother' 'e's goin' ter marry 'er—see? Well, the old girl she don't like it at all, and, of course, she can't say nothink in front of 'is sweet'eart. But after she goes to bed, she gits 'im on his own, and she says to 'im—'don't you be a fool, Robert: you didn't ought ter git married jest yet at all'—yer see she don't want no blinkin' bird comin' between 'er and 'er son and takin' 'im away from 'ome, so she tells 'im to be a good son and drop it. Well, then o' course 'e tells 'er as 'e's got hisself into a mess—and so she says 'My poor boy,' and 'dreadful,' and all the rest, and you hears it—and there ya are—you stand on me, Mary, that's it—she's tryin' ter git 'im to pack it all up, an' 'e won't. Think I don't know?—why the way my mum carried on about the girl I used to go with!—Crikey! Think *I* don't know? all mothers is the same. Only natural you know, after all!"

This profound view of the case was held also by the respective representatives of the various other tradesmen who called that day, and so by the afternoon Mary was convinced that Mrs. Armstrong was "dead against" Robert marrying Dora Owen, and, in view of the authoritative source from which she had received the explanation of what had puzzled her so, and scared her not a little, this conviction of hers could not have been shaken by Mrs. Armstrong herself—or even by the evidence of her own eyes, although, to do her justice, Mary was far too innocent of the ways of the world to understand the whole of the meaning implied by the baker boy's suggestion.

But the maturer intellect and greater experience of the sleepy gardener later proclaimed the affair to be one of much deeper moment than mere maternal antagonism towards a bride to be.

"There's more in it than that," said he, sucking his teeth profoundly, "there's somethin' queer abart this 'ouse . . . ain't you never noticed it? there's been queer goin's on 'ere after dark for a long time past."

Mary was dubious, and so the man gave her greater details.

"You may not know it, Mary," said he, "but Master Robert creeps about the place at night: and it don't mean nothin' good either. What's 'e doin' of, sneaking round in the middle of the night up in that *lavoratory* of his? That's wot I want to know."

"Why he's busy with his experiments, of course," replied Mary. But the gardener shook his head.

"Not he," said that worthy. "He's doing no experiments: or, if he is, then they're experiments wot didn't ought to be allowed. There's something *'orrible* goin' on up there!" And the man pointed with his pipe to the window of Robert's chemical laboratory: "And he ain't alone in the matter either. There's someone with 'im in it all. Someone 'e whispers to, and mutters to—and wot moans and wails in a way that'ud curdle a man's blood."

"Ee lovey, don't be so gruesome," said Mary, "you make me feel frightened."

"And well you may," went on the gardener, warming to his subject, " 'oo is it wot throws a shadow on the curtains up there night after night . . .? And it ain't Master Robert's shadow either . . . it's someone else . . . An' I tells you it wails sometimes, and laughs at others—laughs in a way wot makes a man think of the way they laugh in 'ell . . . It's 'is mother wot's in with 'im, Mary . . . 'is mother wot giggles and carries on so horrible with 'im. But wot do they do up there . . . that's wot I want to know . . . W*ot do they do together all night up in that there room* with them drugs, and them skulls, and that there mummy . . . you caught 'em last night talkin' together—'im and 'is mother . . . well now I knows 'oo it is wot's been up there with 'im all this time . . . it's 'is mother . . . I've watched that winder night after night . . . and seen the shadows on the curtains . . . an' they've done somethin' 'orrible . . . so 'orrible that 'e's frightened to think of wot 'e's been and done . . . and she's scared too to think of 'ow she's 'elped him to do it . . . Look at all them lights all over the 'ouse never orf night or day . . . do you think that's just 'cause they forgets to switch 'em orf . . . 'course it ain't . . . It's because they're frightened . . . frightened to be in the dark for a second . . . frightened to open a cupboard if there's no great blazin' electric light on in it. It's *fear,* that's what it is . . . There's no good never comes out of all this studyin' and ponderin' and peerin' down microscopes . . . an' learnin' things as we wos never meant to know. I'd never stop 'ere a minute longer after wot I see's goin' on only this is such a good job, and it's so difficult to find any work these times. But I wouldn't sleep in the 'ouse for five hundred pounds I wouldn't—straight I wouldn't."

(The gardener, by the way, actually slept in a room built over the stables nearby.)

"It's months, and months, and months ago now since I first got wind of this," he went on to the horrified Mary, who only listened through sheer fascination, "months, and months, it is. I 'ad a bonfire at the bottom of the garden one evenin', burnin' up a lot of old rubbish, and Master Robert 'e must 'ave seen it . . . cause 'e comes down the garden, and goes into the old tool shed . . . you know, Mary, the one wot's never used and 's always locked, and 'e's the only person wot's got the key 'cause it's got all 'is old packing-cases in it wot 'is chemicals come in. Well, 'e goes in there, and 'e starts choppin' up somethin'. I hears 'im and I thinks it only my place to go in there and do it for 'im. So in I goes, and I raises my cap businesslike and says to 'im: 'Pardon me, sir, but 'adent I better do that for you?' . . . well, 'e kind of jumps out of 'is skin, and turns round, and glares at me . 'is 'ands all shakin' and 'is eyes gleamin' . . . frightened to death . . . and wicked with anger and fear.

" 'Get out!' he screamed at me, 'damn you, get out . . . how dare you spy on me?' Streuth! He raises 'is chopper as if 'e'd 'ave 'it me with it. And out I goes all of a tremble, But not before I see wot it wos 'e wos choppin' up. And I've 'ardly 'ad any sleep since . . ."

He lowered his voice suddenly, and, bending down over Mary's fuzzy grey head, continued in a beery whisper,

"It wos shiny, polished, wood . . . there wos bits of brass too . . . all gorn green . . . and it looked like . . . it wos . . . it looked like it wos . . ."

He bent down still lower and wheezed into Mary's ear— his eyes glowing with horrible triumph;

"It looked like it was an old *corfin!*"

Now when Dora Owen had awakened that morning to find the sunlight streaming into the room, and Kathleen sitting up in bed demolishing her fifth banana, she felt quite ashamed of her fears of the previous night, and thoroughly convinced that the yellow face she had seen at the window had been, in reality, no more than a figment of her imagination.

Still, she could hardly help noticing that, not only did Robert seem strange and very restless all day long, to say nothing of looking very tired about the eyes, but there was an indefinable change in Mrs. Armstrong. She seemed as if suddenly she had become unable to look Dora in the face without her glance shifting, and more than once the girl caught her in tears when she thought she was unobserved. Not only so, but the woman appeared terrified at the sound of an unexpected footfall, and, moreover, crept about the place as if fearful of her steps being heard. Her face, usually, despite her comparatively mature years, was as smooth as a child's: but to-day there were strange lines of care about her mouth, and Dora noticed that she twitched all over like one whose nerves were all on edge; and, when she spoke, it was in a low tremulous voice and had a manner suggesting that her mind was far away. She seemed too as if she were listening intently for something she dreaded to hear; and that, far from being relieved at not hearing it, its absence made her apprehension the greater.

Nor indeed were Mrs. Armstrong and Robert the only members of the household in whom Dora noticed this change. Mary the cook, needless to say, had taken the gardener's story very much to heart, and, consequently, was in such a state of befuddlement through "nerves" that she dropped everything she touched. Not only so, but she was frightened out of her wits at the very sight of Mrs. A. and her son, and absolutely unable to disguise the fact.

Now Dora had taken an odd fancy to Mary: partly because she was very old and very kindly: partly because she seemed to be the scapegoat of the family, and Dora pitied her utter incapacity to keep out of trouble. So at the first opportunity she buttonholed the old woman and asked her point-blank what the matter was.

Mary fully reciprocated Dora's liking, voting her "a very sweet girl" and so it did not take much pressing to get her to unbosom herself.

"I'm frightened . . . so . . . so terribly . . . frightened, Miss Dora," she stammered through her chattering teeth, in answer to her enquiry.

"But what about?"

"I don't know . . ."

"But how foolish to be frightened about something and not know what it is," replied Dora gently; and then, as she noticed that the poor old soul was simply shaking with terror from head to foot, she slipped a sheltering arm round her waist.

"Come, Mary," she said gently, "you must not give way like this: it will make you so ill."

"But I can't help it," moaned the trembling woman, "I can't help it."

"But can't you tell me what's troubling you?" continued Dora, imagining, naturally enough, that poor Mary had committed some more than usually terrible domestic offence and was frightened of what might be said to her when it was found out, and remembering a dreadful occasion, some days ago when a ten guinea electric oven had been left full on for a solid week, and had exploded in consequence, and whose lack of memory had been responsible for the tragedy, "surely you can tell me, Mary. You know that I would never breathe a word to a soul. Not only so, but if there's nothing else to be done, and we can't prevent its being found out, I'll say I did it—so there, and then you'll not get into trouble. They'll not say anything to me, I know . . . come on, dear, tell me what's frightening you."

Mary's lip quivered for an instant, and then she burst into tears.

"You're so sweet . . . so kind . . ." she sobbed. "You're the only one who has any pity on me . . . I . . . I . . ." she broke off, trying to get herself a little more under control.

"What is it, dear? . . . what have you done? . . . just whisper and it'll be all right."

"It's not anything I've done that's bothering me," whimpered Mary, "it's something far worse . . . it's . . . it's . . ."

She broke off gasping—and then, recovering herself a little, burst out,

"There's been such eerie, creepy, horrible things happening here!"

"Is that all?" asked Dora, smiling, thinking that Mary had heard about her own fears of the previous night. She knew Kathleen loved to tease the life out of poor old Mary, and thought that there could be little doubt but that she had heard some suitably "doctored" account of the affair from this quarter—what a shame it was!

"Don't let that worry you, you dear old silly," she went on, "that must have been all my imagination. When I thought I saw that face at the laboratory window I was frightened myself I know—that's why I didn't sleep in my own room last night—but now I feel sure that it was only a shadow."

Mary, by the way, knew nothing of Dora's experience; and so, when she learned that a hideous yellow face had actually been seen in the laboratory window and by Dora herself, whom she regarded as the quintessence of common-sense, it is hardly necessary to say that it "put the lid on it."

Her last atom of reserve broke down; and, clinging closely to Dora, like a frightened child, she told her everything.

Bit by bit the story came out: how Mary had seen Robert and his mother creeping upstairs from the dining-room after overhearing those ominous scraps of conversation through the locked door: the opinion of the baker's boy and his colleagues: and finally the gruesome tale told by the gardener.

"And I know I shall never sleep quiet any more," Mary concluded . . . "I've always felt, somehow, that there was something funny about that room of Master Robert's. At first I thought it was only my fancy and the horrid skeletons and things up there. But now I know it's something worse . . . something that will send us all to the madhouse one day . . . What are they doing . . . what are they doing?"

She was all but incoherent with terror.

Dora comforted her as best she could, saying that it was all nonsense and so forth. But, truth to tell, the tale gave her a very nasty shock. For one thing it resuscitated her fears of the previous evening, and made her feel that, after all, possibly, that face had really been in the window, and not merely projected there from her imagination. For another, it seemed to put a barrier of a singularly painful character between her lover and herself.

Of course the whole thing might be mere idle gossip. But, if not, if there should be a basis of truth to the gardener's story, it was evident that there existed a secret—probably a dark one too—in her lover's life which apparently he either could or would not share with her—a secret, moreover, in which it seemed his mother was involved. Dora could not help noticing that since Mrs. Armstrong had learned of her engagement to Robert her manner had changed singularly. And this change was not merely the kind one generally associates with the birth of that commonplace antagonism of a mother jealous of her son's betrothed. She seemed to *fear* something. What could it be? Could it be that she dreaded lest Robert should take his future wife into his confidence?

Had it not been for the fact that Mary had begged and implored her to treat the tale she had told her as strictly confidential, and that she had promised to do so, Dora most certainly would have made an attempt to have the whole matter out then and there, and beseech both her lover and his mother to let her into the secret. As it was, however, she could only hope that Robert would voluntarily take her into his confidence, and she mentally resolved that whatever the mystery should prove, ultimately, to be, her love for, and faith in, the man she had chosen as her life mate should remain unchanged. One thing she felt convinced about and that was, that any guilt in the matter—if guilt there was—could not, and did not, rest on the shoulders of Robert Armstrong.

But her position was a terrible one, and she could not help feeling it very acutely; any more than she was able to prevent herself from constantly turning the thing over in her mind.

Worse still, as time wore on, she felt herself getting more and more frightened. The darker it grew with the approach of night the more sinister the whole thing appeared.

What did it mean? she asked herself over and over again. Who was the owner of that withered yellow face which had stared down so malignantly upon her from the window? She no longer doubted that it had actually been there in all its uncanny horror. Could it be that it had been Mrs. Armstrong watching them from in the rose garden: and, if so, why that terrible glare of hatred. And if not, what was it?

What had been the meaning of that strange midnight meeting between mother and son? It had followed upon her having seen the face. Might it not, therefore, have been a meeting in which they had discussed . . . what?

It was dreadful! Her mind went round and round and round in the matter without getting anywhere at all. How bitterly she regretted the promise she had made Mary, and how terribly she longed to speak to somebody about it all, although something in the bottom of her heart told her that to do so might put her in possession of something she would rather not know.

Robert, in spite of his restlessness, nervy manner and exhaustion which Dora had noticed hanging over him the whole day through, was as devoted a lover as ever, and continued at every opportunity to press for an early marriage.

"Why not let me go to London to-morrow and buy a special license?" he had asked, "then we can be married to-morrow."

"But, darling," rejoined Dora, "what about *my* clothes—really I ought to go home for a week or so first and get everything ready."

"Never mind clothes," he replied, "what do they matter? besides I'll buy you anything you want—only do marry me quickly and let us get away from this place—it tears my nerves to pieces."

Dora was on the point of partly confiding her own fears to him by bringing up again the matter of the yellow face: but, somehow, although the words were on the tip of her tongue, she held them back—probably because of a subconscious instinct that the knowledge of the dark secret she felt sure was hanging over "Restormal" would be more than she could bear—worse, possibly, than the vague terror which weighed her down.

"We must get away from here together and start life anew somewhere," went on Robert, "I can't stand this place much longer."

Dora threw out a feeler without being able to help herself.

"But, Robert dearest, it's your own home, and it's a beautiful old place."

"Yes, yes, I know that," he replied, with a shade of irritation. "But it's dark, and old, and gloomy, and it depresses me beyond words: do let us find some cheerful little home where we can leave the shadows of the past behind us."

"Shadows of the past dear, what shadows?"

But he ignored her question, and continued:—

"Surely you don't want to live here—surely there can be no attraction for you m this wearisome old place?"

"No, dear," she replied gently, "not if you would prefer somewhere else: but what about your laboratory—do you think you'll be able to find anywhere small with a room large enough to hold all your instruments and apparatus?"

"I'm not going to trouble about that," he broke in. "If necessary, I can arrange for the use of a laboratory in London and carry out my experiments there: and, as to transferring my laboratory, I don't intend to bring my work into our home. I've had enough of it. I can go to London twice or three times a week and that will have to do. I want home to be a place of refuge, rest, and peace. Don't you agree with me that it should be?"

"Of course, dearest," answered the girl, wondering more than ever what could be afoot, "but I always regarded you as being absorbed in your work—has something turned you against it?"

"Never mind that now," he replied, "all I want to think of now is our future home, and just how quickly we can find it."

He seemed quite obsessed with the desire to leave "Restormal" at the earliest possible moment, and continued to worry for a speedy wedding, until, at last, when Dora retired for the night, it had been arranged that she should write home the very next day and summon her parents to attend the ceremony at the local church that day week.

Dora could not sleep. Her mind was full of gloomy forebodings and half-formed terror. Robert's painful anxiety to get away from "Restormal" at all costs and as quickly as possible confirmed those dread suspicions which had been aroused by all that she had heard. It was no mere idle servants' gossip—the links in the chain held together far too well for that. Right from the first moment of her visit, Dora had doubted if forgetfulness could altogether account for those myriad fights which blazed night and day in every room, passage, nook and cranny of that old, rambling, isolated house; and now she began to realise that the true cause was not absent-mindedness but *fear*—desperate *fear* of any part of the house being in darkness even for an instant. There was, beyond doubt, some dark secret hanging over the household, and over Robert in particular. But what could it be? what could it be? That was the question which kept the girl on the rack.

She twisted and turned restlessly on her bed, quite unable to settle down comfortably for more than a few minutes at a time, wondering, puzzling, and pondering the while.

The more she puzzled, the more frightened she became, as the pure mystery of the affair wore off somewhat to be replaced by its gruesome features. With a sick shudder she remembered how the gardener—according to Mary—had caught Robert in the very act of chopping up an old coffin at the bottom of the garden many, many, months ago. What could that mean? Had the man seen aright, and, if so, how came Robert into possession of a coffin, and why did he desire to destroy it? Then again, that yellow face had looked down on to the garden from the laboratory window: and Robert had seemed strangely unwilling to go near the place since. Not only so, but he had actually suggested that he desired to use it no longer.

Why? What had brought about this sudden change?

It seemed, in fact, as if there was something in that laboratory that he feared: but if so, what could it be, and why had the fear suddenly come about.

It seemed to date from the appearance of that yellow face at the window . . .

And more, Mrs. Armstrong was in Robert's confidence. His mother was involved . . . and she had changed more amazingly than her son since the appearance of that face.

Again, why? Again that agonised question . . . that question to which Dora could find no answer.

What unnamable horror was in that house? In what dark and terrible secret were mother and son united? What dangers lurked in that strange room of mysteries? What unspoken fear made the entire household dread a moment of darkness?

A thousand horrible possibilities floated before the girl's mind. Possessed of a powerful imagination, she thought, and imagined, and dreamed herself into a state of utter terror, wishing heartily the while that she had shared Kathleen's room, as she had done the night before, instead of sleeping— or rather trying to sleep—alone in this great gloomy room with a mind haunted by shapeless terrors.

Utterly worn out at last she sank into a troubled sleep, although only to wake up with a jump about every ten minutes, wonder in heartsick terror what had aroused her, and then drop off again.

Even when, finally, she did sink into a really deep slumber, it was *only* to be haunted by dreams: formless dreams of unmeaning horror which made her long for wakefulness once more.

What a mockery sleep is sometimes. How often, while the body is lying in repose, does the brain writhe in the anguish of the dreams by which it is tormented. How utterly then does sleep often fail as a refuge for a troubled mind, often doing nothing more than binding the body down in darkness and silence that the soul may concentrate upon those things by which in wakefulness it was troubled. How thankful are we then, sometimes, to wake: thinking perchance in shuddering of sleep's twin sister—death, from whose lethargy there is *no* awakening: and dreading lest the "hell of fire" may prove to be the dreams tormenting those wrapped in the sleep everlasting—dreams which must go on for all eternity.

Dora dreamed first that she was swinging in a starlit garden, and that Robert propelled the swing: that he swung her too high, and that she entreated him to be more gentle. But it was useless: no sooner had she descended than she was swung into the air again with greater force than before: to descend in an anguished fear of being dashed to pieces.

Heaven be praised! She was unhurt though badly shaken. But—horror, Oh horror—yet again she was driven upwards: again, again, and again, in anguish and in terror, till, at last, she thought she lost hold of the swing thousands of feet above the sleeping city . . .

Where was she? . . . She was still ascending . . . but she suddenly found herself climbing stairs . . . hundreds of them . . . narrow, winding, stairs . . . where could she be?

Why, of course, how stupid of her not to have remembered, she was climbing up those deserted stairs which led to Robert's laboratory.

Up, up, up. Oh what a way it was: it seemed as though she would never get there. But, at last, she found her hand on the door knob: at last she entered that dream-room to find it illuminated by a greenish flickering light, and to see Robert bending over his work.

In her dream she spoke his name, and she saw him turn round and face her.

God of Pity! What had happened to him. The flesh of his face had withered away: it was not a human countenance that he turned towards her but a grinning skull—a skull from the bony orbits of which shone two menacing *eyes.*

And then through the subterranean night of dreams came his voice.

"Back!" it shouted, "back from this place: here you may not enter: for here is that upon which you durst not look: here is the living death!"

Dora awoke in a cold sweat. God in Heaven, what a dream! But was it over yet? Was she indeed awake?

She must be. She was lying in bed just as she had been when she fell asleep. But, somehow, the room didn't seem quite the same as it had been before that awful dream. She had a feeling that she was no longer alone: she sensed a *presence* somewhere in the silent darkness.

A presence . . . a presence . . .

Yes, there *was* someone in the room—of that she felt certain. Somewhere in the still blackness she could hear *breathing,* while the door creaked a little on its hinges. It must have been opened while she lay asleep bound hand and foot by those hellish dreams. She had made sure it was fast closed before retiring.

In a sudden panic Dora sat right up in bed. The next instant she opened her lips to utter one strangled scream of terror.

Standing at the foot of the bed, silhouetted against the feeble greyish glimmer of faint moonlight through thick clouds which illuminated her window, was a human figure. It looked like a woman, for long, straight, dead white hair hung loose over the shoulders, and, although Dora could not see the face, she *felt*,—felt distinctly,—two glaring eyes full of hatred fixed upon her.

Almost at the same instant there was a sudden rush and clatter of feet from outside her room, and the door burst open to admit Robert. He was fully dressed, and without seeming to realise the presence of Dora, made straight for the foot of the bed, springing with a strangled oath upon the woman there like a wild beast at its prey, and dragging her fighting and struggling across the carpet and out of the door.

Dora lay on the bed scarcely daring to breathe, listening in horror to the curses and scuffling which sounded as though Robert were dragging or rather, trying to drag the woman either up or down a flight of stairs, and gradually became muffled by distance.

Hour upon hour Dora lay there, trembling like an aspen leaf: frightened at the beating of her own heart: too terrified to move a limb or an eyelid: incapable of coherent thought, until the first pale grey streaks of early dawn began to filter through her window when her worn out body overcame her fear-paralysed mind and she dropped off into a heavy doze through which, very dimly, she thought she could hear the sound of a distant commotion.

The next thing she knew was that it was broad daylight and the morning sun was streaming into the room, while someone was hammering impatiently at her door.

When at last, feeling dizzy and sick, she forced herself to answer this insistent summons, it was to learn that the police were in possession of the house.

Mrs. Armstrong had been *murdered* in the night.

CHAPTER IV

MR. JACK SEAGAR THE GARDENER at "Restormal" to whom we have been introduced already in an earlier chapter, was a gentleman who held rather strong political opinions which led him to resent very much indeed the state of affairs making it necessary for him to "garden" for hire (i.e. go to sleep in a wheelbarrow) during the greater part of every day, while the family employing him were privileged to "five in a big 'ouse," and "do just as they blinkin' well liked" at all times and seasons. Being, at the same time, one of those individuals who hold, as an article of faith, that people who possess money in any quantity must either have made it, or be making it, by professional crime, he suspected that the Armstrongs were crooks, and determined that one fine day he would "find them out"—purely, of course, from a high sense of public duty, though he did happen to dislike heartily anybody who chanced to be richer than he, and the occupants of "Restormal" in particular.

And so when he actually discovered that there really was "something 'orrible" going on in the place, his long-nursed suspicion became an absolute certainty, and he made it his business from that very moment to keep an exceptionally careful watch upon the internal economy of the household by night when it seemed to him the 'orrible things in question generally took place, determining with all the instinct of a born Sherlock Holmes to run the whole mystery to earth, if only to show everybody concerned—and for the matter of that everybody not concerned as well—that he had been right from the very beginning in his estimate of his employers' true character.

Finally, when he heard from Mary the cook of how Robert's engagement to Dora Owen—according to the baker's boy's opinion (a detail, by the way, Mary forgot to mention)—did not meet with the whole-hearted approval of Mrs. Armstrong, and was told of the strange midnight meeting between mother and son, his genius for criminal detection sensed that the dark doings, whatever they might turn out to be, were about to come to a head, and so that particular night he kept an unceasing vigil on the perpetually illuminated windows.

It was a very still night, its darkness relieved only by the most pale and watery of moons peering dimly through horizontal layers of ragged clouds, when Mr. Seagar donned his heavy boots and overcoat, locked up his private premises over the disused stables, picked up a thick stick for protection if need be, and trudged out on his self-imposed mission of running what he considered to be a dangerous gang to earth.

In spite of the great public importance of his errand, we may as well confess that Mr. Seagar did not seem altogether easy in his mind: for one thing his teeth chattered audibly although it could hardly be called a cold night and he was muffled up as if for a polar expedition, and for another he kept on glancing furtively behind him as though fearful that he might be followed.

The garden certainly did look very eerie in the oddly-diffused moonlight. Two huge fir-trees grew on either side of the rustic archway leading into the rose-garden and cast tall shadows on the grass, swaying dismally to and fro in the midnight breeze, while every time little gusts of wind caught the myriad leaves of the thick foliage round about, there came a rustling like the whispering of many tongues.

Stark against the mackerel sky was outlined the blasted trunk of a great tree that had been struck by lightning from which projected two withered branches looking horribly like a pair of sinister arms. In the far distance could be heard the hooting of owls, while now and again a great bat swirled across the deep blue sky towards "Restormal" as though attracted by some evil influence from within, heavy black storm clouds gathering into a threatening pall over the great house from every window of which blazed forth light.

Now although as a rule light is considered as an antidote to fear, there was something vaguely terrifying about those great deserted rooms being so fiercely illuminated at that unearthly hour, and as he took his stand behind a high privet hedge, Mr. Seagar felt that his situation was unbearably horrible.

Hardly had he settled there when his attention was immediately arrested by a light appearing suddenly in the one dark window in the whole house—that odd little dormer window jutting out of the roof which belonged to the laboratory—a glimmering greenish light like dim prolonged lightning, and across the blind passed the shadow of a woman.

"Ah!" thought the gardener, grasping his stick, "that's the old girl—she's at it—now something's sure to happen."

And before ten minutes had passed happen something did too: a woman's piercing scream rang out into the night: a blood-curdling shriek of pain mingled with a terrible fear.

Mr. Jack Seagar had never been remarkable for his courage: it had been curiosity born of sub-conscious class antagonism more than anything else that had brought him out. He had hoped certainly that something would happen in the nature of say some member of the establishment setting out on a cat burglaring expedition which he could have followed or a confab of crooks taking place where he could have overheard some deep plot to rob the Bank of England: but as to anything coming about such as that dreadful scream suggested even to his rather second-rate imagination—well that was quite another thing, and had he even dreamed of such a thing happening he would have been conspicuous by his absence, that's all.

As it was, however, he *felt* his hair rising, and cold sweat trickling down his back. Horrors! Suppose someone had been *murdered*! And the murderer were to come out, and see *him* . . . You can only hang a man once, and a killer would certainly not hesitate to spill blood a second time if his own chance of escape depended upon it. And then Mr. Seagar remembered something. He remembered that "old corfin" he had seen Robert chopping up at the bottom of the garden in that old abandoned tool-shed, *blimey*! Suppose it *had been* a coffin *really*! (you see, in point of fact it had only *looked* like one, and Mr. Seagar, in order to impress Mary with the importance of his discovery and his powers of observation, had exaggerated a little).

Blimey! It *must* have been a *real* coffin! Visions of fame, sense of Public duty, curiosity, self-importance, and even his own high opinion of himself as a Sherlock Holmes, all evaporated on the spot, and Mr. Jack Seagar adopted the better part of valour.

In fact to put it bluntly, he *ran away* as fast as his trembling legs could carry him.

Naturally enough, the direction he took led well away from the house—he would have done anything rather than have gone an inch nearer the point from whence came that dreadful scream. Dashing through the hedge he rushed anglewise across the croquet lawn to the garden boundary wall, tore through the foliage and scrambled hell for leather over the top: an acrobatic feat which in cold blood he could no more have done than fly, cutting his hands rather badly in the process on the array of broken bottles which it boasted.

The other side of that particular wall was a lane, and down the lane at that precise moment, were walking two policemen homeward bound after their day's work at a certain traffic control point not far off.

Now when these two limbs of the law saw a burly man come tumbling over a wall out of private property at the witching hour of 2 A.M. and in a manner distinctly suggesting that all hell—or rather all the household—were after him, they obviously mistook him for one of their natural prey in the concluding phases of a professional expedition; and so, with a view holloa, collared him on the spot.

Witness their amazement when their prisoner registered the wildest joy at being "copped" so neatly, and clinging with gory hands to their regulation overcoats, gasped out,

"Quick—quick—guv'nor—murder—murder—there's people bein' *murdered* in that there 'ouse."

Five minutes later, the constables, in company with Mr. Seagar, who was shaking from head to foot in utter terror, had forced one of the front windows of "Restormal" and climbed in.

They landed in the dining-room, which was flooded with light from a huge electric chandelier, and, seeing at a glance that it was absolutely empty, made their way out into the great hall.

Here again every available lamp was burning, but no one could be seen, and they drew blank at each and every room they entered although all of them absolutely blazed with light.

At last they threw open the door of the largest bedroom, and there what a sight met their eyes.

The room was palatially furnished in genuine Chippendale, and brilliantly illuminated by two electric "rise and fall" fittings, one of which hung over the bed. This was a heavy black four poster, and had apparently not been slept in that night, since its spotless down quilt and expensive linen were undisturbed.

Lying across the bed in a strained and horribly unnatural attitude was an elderly woman. She was stone dead, and her face—as far as it could be seen through the great masses of long white hair which smothered it, the tresses of which were literally gummed together by bloodclots—was drawn into such an expression of mingled fear and hatred that it horrified even the hard-boiled policemen. As to Mr. Seagar, he just gasped out, "Mrs. Armstrong, by the Lord!"—and tried to bolt headlong from the room, although unsuccessfully, as the police were too quick for him.

The woman seemed to have been stabbed to death, for there was a dreadful gash in her throat from which trickled a sticky red ribbon of gore, and lying nearby in a pool of blood was a narrow bladed Indian dagger.

It was a sensational case. In the whole of Detective-Inspector Bradfield's forty years' criminal practice he could recall nothing quite like it. And the features of the tragedy really were very singular. That great house with its every room flooded with light in the small hours of the morning: its master away in the Provinces—exactly where nobody seemed to know save his wife who lay stabbed to death in a pool of blood, on her own bed: the whole of the rest of the household paralysed with fear, all refusing point-blank to go anywhere near the body save Robert, her son, for the identification of which he had, therefore, to depend almost entirely upon the word of one man, and all babbling forth stories of vaguely horrible improbabilities, presented him with a problem to solve which, to say the least of it, was pretty tough, when, summoned by telephone, he motored down to "Restormal" from Scotland Yard.

But tough problems are the paving stones of the path leading to fame for the criminal investigator: and so the detective, although puzzled, was by no means displeased by what he found, and buckled to with a will in the matter of elucidating the mystery.

He made the dining-room his headquarters, and having carefully examined the dagger with which the crime had been committed, and then sent it off for expert examination by finger-print specialists asking at the same time for photographs of any prints which might come to fight underneath the great gouts and clots of blood with which the weapon was so thickly covered from end to end, instructed the constables he had brought down with him to get the entire household together in another room and bring them before him one by one.

Learning from the two local policemen the way in which the crime had first come to fight, Bradfield started his examination with the gardener, who had previously been identified by the horrified Kathleen.

"Now, Mr. Seagar," said he, when the trembling and dazed amateur sleuth was brought before him—"you were seen by P.C. Fisher and P.O. Heartly climbing over the side wall of this house at 2.05 A.M. this morning. When arrested on suspicion, you told the constables that there was murder being done in the house, did you not?"

"Yessir."

"How did you know that there was murder being done?"

"I heard an 'orrible scream, sir."

"I see. Where were you when you heard this scream?"

"In the garden, sir."

"Do you do your gardening by night then?"

"No, sir."

"Well, then, what were you doing in the garden at two in the morning?"

Seagar hesitated, and then said,

"I was watching this 'ouse."

"Why?"

"'Cause I thought 'twas my duty."

"And why did you think it was your duty?"

Once more the man hesitated for an instant—and then, seeing no doubt an opportunity of getting himself into the limelight as a star witness, he took on a kind of man to man, confidential tone, and said,

"I've seen this 'ere murder comin' for a long time past—a long time past."

Bradfield pricked up his ears.

"You have, have you—in what way?"

"There's been strange goin's on in this 'ouse: goin's on wot can only lead to murders—and maybe this ain't the first murder either."

"What do you mean: not the first murder? Speak up man."

Mr. Seagar did, and regaled the detective with the tale he had told to Mary—although he found the Scotland Yard man rather a "hard audience"—to use an actor's term. In fact, had it not been for the concrete tragedy he was investigating, Bradfield would most certainly have discounted every word on the spot—as it was he determined to sift it to the bottom.

"Will you *swear* upon Oath that it was a coffin you saw Robert Armstrong chopping up?" was his first question, adding sharply, "and please bear in mind that every word you say is being taken down as evidence."

Mr. Seagar looked uncomfortable, bit his lip, and shifted from one foot to the other uneasily, so to encourage him a little, the detective remarked:

"Finally, don't forget that to conceal anything you know is a serious offence. It *might*, in fact, involve you in the crime itself should the facts you suppressed come to fight of themselves and turn out to have a vital bearing on the case."

Here was a pretty cleft stick to get out of. The gardener did not like it at all, and wished he had not played the spy. But it was no good wishing now, and so he said,

"Well, sir—it was a long box made of shiny wood, and there wos brass 'andles there too—and then Mr. Robert's manner . . . you'd 'ave thought 'e'd 'ave killed me he was that frightened and angry."

"I see. And he burned the chopped up pieces on a bonfire?"

"Yessir."

"Did you look for the handles in that shed or in the ashes of the fire—they could not have been burned you know."

"No, sir. There was no trace of them 'andles."

"Did you look for them?"

"Yes."

Bradfield made a note or two, and continued:

"You tell me this was months and months ago—just when, actually, was it?"

"About a year ago—I can't remember exactly, sir . . . but it was just about this time of the year, sir . . ."

"Humph!" grunted Bradfield. "Well, we'll let that rest. You say you have frequently seen the dead woman and her son together at night?"

"Yessir—I'll swear to that, sir—I've seen the shadow of 'er long white 'air, sir—on the blind of that there *lavoratory* many and many a night."

"Lavoratory?"

"Mr. Robert's room up yonder where he does all 'is experiments."

"Laboratory, you mean, of course."

"Yessir."

"Robert Armstrong is a scientist, of course."

"Yessir."

"Do you know if his mother was very interested in his work?"

"No, sir—she was sort of proud of him—but that's all."

"Were they much together during the day as well?"

"No, sir—Mr. Robert was up there alone, and Mrs. Armstrong always in the garden. That I'll vouch for, sir."

"But at night—after everyone had retired she was frequently up in his workroom?"

"Yes."

"Might it not have been some other woman?"

"No, sir."

"Not his fiancée, for instance?"

"No, sir—it couldn't 'ave been Miss Dora because I see that shadow on the blind long before she was 'ere."

"I see—is there any other woman in the household besides Mrs. Armstrong?"

No, sir—that is not with long 'air sir—there's only Mary the cook, and 'er 'air's frizzy and very short—and she's short too 'erself that is. And she and Mrs. Armstrong was the only women who slept in the place till Miss Dora came to stay."

"Did you ever see more than the silhouette the blind?"

"No, sir."

"And this silhouette resembled Mrs. Armstrong in every way?"

"Yessir."

"And you tell me that Mary the cook confided to you that she had actually seen Mrs. Armstrong herself with her son under strange circumstances one night quite recently."

"Yessir."

"When did you first see the shadow of the woman you insist was Mrs. Armstrong on the laboratory blind?"

Seagar considered for a while—then his face lighted up as if an idea had struck him, and he replied,

"Why, so 'elp me, Inspector, it was just the very night after I see Mr. Robert burnin' that old corfin. That made me suspicious and I watched the 'ouse—and I saw 'em together for the first time then—about three in the mornin'."

"But until that night you had not watched the laboratory window at all?"

"No."

"So you do not actually know that this was the first time the woman's shadow appeared on the blind?"

"It was the first time I saw it."

"No doubt: but since you had never watched the window before it could hardly have failed to be."

The gardener saw the force of the argument and kept silence. Bradfield's next question was,

"Since when have the lights in this house been kept burning day and night?"

"As long as I can remember."

"Thank you, Mr. Seagar. Just one more question. Your full name is—"

"James Seagar, sir."

"And how long have you been gardener here?"

"Three years, sir."

"And during that time you have always slept outside the house?"

"Yessir—I used to be in lodgings until Mr. Armstrong give me them two rooms over the garage there."

"Thank you. That will be all for the moment," said the Inspector, and Mr. Seagar shuffled from the room thankful to have escaped from the detective.

Bradfield determined that the next person to be brought before him should be Mary the cook, who, by this time, was in as fit a condition to be questioned as she was likely to be for many a long day to come. The murder had upset her nerves so terribly, though, that when at last she could be persuaded to accompany the policeman into the dining-room where the detective was interrogating each member of the household separately as was his wont, she had to be all but carried there.

The Inspector eyed the huddled heap with more than a touch of pity, had her put into one of the arm chairs, and then said very gently.

"I'm very sorry to have to send for you as I can see you have had a very dreadful shock. But it is absolutely necessary that I ask you one or two questions which may help in clearing up this tragedy—although you can set your mind at rest because nobody suspects you personally of being in the least connected with it. Still you are a member of the household, and you might be able to give me some useful information."

"But who could have murdered Mrs. Armstrong—who—who—" moaned poor Mary.

"That is just what we want to find out," said Bradfield. "So do try to pull yourself together—just for a few minutes, and answer me very carefully."

"I'm so frightened . . ."

"There's nothing whatever to be frightened about. Now try to think . . . when did you last see poor Mrs. Armstrong alive?"

"It was about . . . ten o'clock . . ."

"Where was she?"

"In the dining-room . . . in here . . ."

"What was she doing?"

"Pacing up and down."

"She seemed upset about something, did she?"

"Well perhaps just a little . . .

"Why did you come in here?"

"I was going to bed, and I just wanted to ask her if she had done with me for to-night."

"So upon leaving her you went straight to bed?"

"Yes."

"What was the first you heard of the trouble?"

"I heard a scream . . . a terrible scream . . ."

"What did you do then?"

"I put my head under the bedclothes."

"And then."

"The scream came again . . . only louder . . . I got out of bed and I locked the door . . . and the next I knew was that there were voices downstairs . . . and the policeman fetched me down, and told me that Mrs. Armstrong had been murdered."

"Thank you. Now, the gardener tells me that two members of this household are in the habit of wandering about the place at night, and that you actually came face to face with them recently, and identified them as the dead woman and her son. Is that a fact?"

"Yes."

"When was it you did so?"

"The night before last."

"How came you to do so?"

"I was worrying because I thought I'd left on the gas, and I came downstairs to see . . . just to make sure . . . the dining-room door was closed and I saw from underneath the door that the gas had been left on . . . and as I knew that they would be sure to lay the blame on me I—"

"The *gas* on in the dining-room . . . what gas? This is the room isn't it?"

"Yes."

"But there is no gas of any sort here."

"Well you know what I mean . . . the light I never can remember . . . my poor head, you know . . ."

"You mean you saw the electric light on from under the door?"

"That's right."

"Well, carry on with your tale."

"I thought I'd better put it off, and when I went to open the door I found it was locked . . . and I heard voices from inside.

"The voices of Mrs. Armstrong and her son?"

"Yes."

"Did you hear what they said?"

"I wouldn't for shame to listen outside a door . . ." began Mary indignantly. But the detective cut her short.

"No one suggests that you intended to overhear the conversation but did you or did you not *happen* to catch a few words: you may speak in absolute confidence."

"Well I did happen to hear a word or two—it was so very quiet you know."

"What did you hear?"

"I heard poor dear Mrs. Armstrong say to Master Robert ... 'poor boy' ... 'terrible' ... and 'death' ..."

"You caught the words, 'terrible' and 'death'?"

"Yes."

"That all you heard?"

"Yes ... but I was only there a very little time before the door was unlocked and they came out of the room."

"What did you do then?"

"I felt frightened and hid behind some curtains until they had passed."

"Where did they go?"

"Upstairs."

"What made you feel frightened?"

"I don't know ... It was all so gruesome somehow."

"What did you do then?"

"I waited until I thought they had gone to bed, and then I went back to my own room."

"You saw no more of them or heard no more of them?"

"No."

"And they did not see you?"

"Oh no."

"Is this the only occasion you have seen or heard anything of people creeping about the house in the night?"

"Yes—but the gardener . . . Mr. Seagar you know . . . says . . ."

"I know all about what he says . . . I've had his whole story long ago . . . have you *personally* heard anything or seen anybody except on the occasion you have just mentioned?"

"No."

"You referred just now to having left the lights on . . . and said that what worried you, apparently was that even if somebody else had left a light on you would be blamed. Now the gardener tells me that every light in the house is left on day and night . . . is that so?"

"Yes . . . you know the lights are often on all night, and Mr. Armstrong goes mad when he gets the bills from the electric people."

"And you say everybody blames you . . . do you leave them on?"

"Sometimes I forget . . . my poor head you know . . . but even if I haven't left a light on and they find it burning they still blame me."

"Too bad. And so you are certain that other people leave the lights on more frequently than you do?"

"Oh yes: and do you know, sometimes I feel sure that they have left them on purposely—just to get the chance to have a fling at me."

"And Mr. Armstrong himself never leaves them on when he is at home?"

"Oh no. He's a most careful man: but all the same, whether he's at home or not, the lights are always left on just the same, and I'm sure it's just to get me into trouble with the master that they leave them on. You see I never can remember."

"A great shame, Mary, a great shame: now, I suppose you don't know where your master is now?"

"No . . . he is away somewhere."

"How long has he been gone?"

"A week."

"Are he and Mrs. Armstrong on good terms?"

"Oh yes—they adore each other . . . and now, poor fellow . . . when he comes home to find . . ."

Mary nearly broke down, and Bradfield waited until she had mastered her emotion a little. Then he continued.

"Do you know when he is expected home?"

"No."

"The gardener tells me that Mr. Robert Armstrong has just got engaged to Miss Dora Owen, a guest in this house, and that according to you Mrs. Armstrong opposes the match—is that so? Have you any reason to think that his mother objects to their engagement?"

"Well you know, lovey, Mr. Wells says that—"

"Who is Mr. Wells?"

"The gentleman who brings the bread round."

"You mean the baker's boy?"

"Yes . . . but he's *such* a nice fellow . . ."

"Carry on."

"Well, Mr. Wells says that the reason Mrs. Armstrong and Master Robert had that long talk together in here the other night was that she didn't like his engagement.

"How did he know of this 'long talk'? I suppose you told him all about it?"

"Yes."

"And that was the opinion he expressed was it . . .?"

"Yes."

"Have you any other reason for this belief as to Mrs. Armstrong's objection to the engagement?"

"No."

"Thank you. And your full name is . . ."

"Mary West."

"How long have you been cook here?"

"Twelve years."

"That will do then . . . You may go.

Mary went accordingly, and Bradfield told the constable on duty to bring forward Dora Owen.

CHAPTER V

DORA STAGGERED INTO THE ROOM. Her head was spinning round, and she felt dazed and ill. A murder committed within a few yards of where she had lain sleeping! And the victim her own hostess: her tentative mother-in-law! It was too awful!

Many a time she had read reports of such tragedies in the newspapers, and shuddered at the vision conjured up in her mind by the story in cold, dead, print—little dreaming that the time would come when she would be actually in the very midst of the grim, concrete reality of violent death: in the very house of crime itself: and subject to the merciless inquisition of the police as, at the best, a source of evidence, and, at the worst, a suspect.

And yet she might almost have suspected that some such horror was brewing in the household when she had seen that face so full of unearthly hatred glaring down upon her that night when she had consented to become Robert's wife. She felt absolutely certain that it had been no hallucination, but a dreadful, stark reality. And, if so, to whom had it belonged? That it had been the face of a woman she knew from the halo of white hair which had surrounded it. The question was—could that woman have been Mrs. Armstrong?—and if not who was she?

She remembered that Mrs. Armstrong had actually been in the house at the moment the face had appeared. She remembered, also, the insincerity which she had caught sight of behind the woman's outward suavity of manner, and how pointedly she had asked what they had been doing in the rose-garden that evening—almost as if she knew what had taken place: and the strange nervousness of both Robert and his mother when she had told them she had seen the face at the window.

Then again there was the powerful link of sympathy she had known to exist between mother and son: Mary's tale of how she had seen them together in the watches of the night apparently discussing something very earnestly: how Mary had actually caught the words "poor boy": and then how the gardener had declared that Robert and his mother used to spend whole nights together in the laboratory: the local opinion that Mrs. Armstrong objected to her son's thinking of marriage: and Robert's insistence that they should have an early marriage and make their home somewhere right away from "Restormal" to say nothing of the odd way in which he seemed to have lost interest in his scientific studies.

And then—coming on top of all this was her terrible experience of that very night: her nightmare: her awakening: that presence in the room which she felt certain had been a woman: Robert's sudden entry and his violence in dragging her out—as if she had intended some harm to Dora.

Who had crept into her room while she had been asleep, and been dragged out like that?

That whoever it was had meant her no good she felt certain: and, moreover, equally sure that Robert must have been on the look out for something of the kind—so rapid had been his appearance on the scene.

And now that almost immediately after this frightening episode—or was it a narrow escape?—Mrs. Armstrong herself discovered dead—stabbed—*murdered* in her bedroom only a few doors away from Dora's room.

Could it not be fearfully possible that Mrs. Armstrong had been the woman who entered her room in the night to do her some dreadful injury, and that Robert, in defence of his bride, to be, had fought with and slain—his own mother?

Frightful, sickening thought!—*matricide*—the crime of *Nero!*

Robert was incapable of such a deed, surely! But then, might it not be possible that he had not seen exactly who it was he attacked?

No—for she remembered hearing the scuffling out in the landing, and there, as in the victim's room, fights were blazing.

But surely he could not have done it: surely fate would not have been so cruel.

There *must* be some other explanation.

But what other explanation would cover the facts?

Robert himself had been brought down from his room by one of the policemen to await examination by Bradfield, and although Dora had begged for an explanation of the strange happenings of the night he had resolutely refused to speak a word beyond saying,

"Whatever it is, it will all come out in the end."

And when she referred to what had taken place in her room, he told her very quietly that she must have been dreaming. But his words were belied by a strange shadow which passed across his eyes as he spoke.

Was it fear? And, if so, fear of what?—that the truth should come to light?

Why—that would mean, surely, his *guilt*. And then, if he had really murdered his mother would it not have been in her defence? Mrs. Armstrong, then, must have come to her room to do something terrible—to kill her perhaps—out of jealousy for her son's affection.

One thing Dora felt was certain—and that was that if Robert had done this terrible thing it had been an accident. He was incapable of committing murder she *knew* as only a woman can know anything—by *intuition*, which is stronger than any logic and nearly any evidence.

But how could this knowledge save him from being hanged as a murderer? The relentless machinery of justice would probe the matter to the bottom, and, in all probability, claim him as its victim. Even though the whole affair rested upon nothing more than just damning circumstantial evidence, the gallows was pretty certain to be the outcome.

But stay—why was she to be examined as a witness? Was it not because they thought that she might reveal something which would lead to the arrest of the killer?

And she actually *did* know something: was not her waking nightmare enough to put a rope round Robert's neck in view of what had followed so swiftly.

Her lover's fate was, to some extent, in her hands. Merciful powers! Suppose it had been so ordained that her own lips—yet warm from his kisses—were to send him to the scaffold—perhaps, too, quite undeservedly!

Suppose—suppose she withheld what she knew? Would it do any good? Had that midnight scuffle been heard by Mary or by the gardener, and referred to in their previous interrogation? If only she could know exactly what the detective had heard from these first two witnesses! What a nerve-racking business it was not to know. Why must the Inspector take them separately—why not allow them to hear each other's story?

But, anyway, it was quite possible that there had as yet been no mention made of that terrible visitant to her room—or rather to the struggle which followed. Mary slept on another floor far away from her (Dora's) room, and the gardener—who slept outside the house—could hardly have heard anything of the scuffle.

And even if they *had* heard it—did they know that it originated in her bedroom?

Dare she withhold anything? Dare she?

All these thoughts, although they seemed to take an eternity to the mind-tortured girl in whose brain they were passing—actually occupied only the space of a few seconds, and were roughly broken into by Detective-Inspector Bradfield's sharp inquiry,

"You are Dora Owen?"

Dora pulled herself together and answered in the affirmative.

"You are engaged to Robert Armstrong, the son of the deceased?"

"Yes."

"And staying here as a guest?"

"Yes."

"By whose invitation?"

"The invitation of Mr. James Armstrong—Robert's father, you know."

"I see. You don't know where Mr. James Armstrong is now, do you?"

"No—that is—I understood him to say he was going to several Provincial Towns."

"Did he mention any in particular?"

"Not to me. Poor Mrs. Armstrong knew though, I believe."

"How long have you been staying here?"

"About a fortnight."

"When did you become engaged to Robert Armstrong?"

"The night before last."

"Are you of full age?"

"I am twenty-two."

"Did Mrs. Armstrong know of your engagement?"

"Oh yes."

"And how did she take it?"

"She just congratulated us and wished us every happiness."

"Have you any reason to believe that she was not sincere in her well wishing?"

So far everything had been quite straightforward. But now it looked as if the questions were steering on to dangerous ground. "What makes him ask this?" thought Dora to herself. "Evidently either Mary or the gardener or both have told him that there was a suggestion that she disliked our engagement." So, in spite of herself, she coloured somewhat as she made answer:

"Of course not . . . why should she?"

"I'll tell you," said Bradfield; "according to the account of the cook and the gardener, there was something rather strange in the relationship between the dead woman and her son. It not only appears that they were in the habit perpetually of walking about the house and frequenting Robert Armstrong's laboratory at extraordinary hours of the night. Not only so, but the cook actually recognised Mrs. Armstrong and her son the very night following your engagement, and it seems that they were having a very serious talk about something in this very room behind locked doors in the dead of night, and the mother seemed to be expressing great sympathy for the son. Further, according to the cook, it transpires that on this very night when you were with Robert Armstrong in the garden, you personally saw a woman looking down on you from the laboratory window, and her expression, it seems according to the statement you are said to have made to the cook, was one of hatred. Now is it a fact you saw such a face on that night?"

"Yes."

"And did you recognise it as anyone?"

"No."

"But you saw the expression on the face: surely you must have been able to tell then whose face it was—or if it was someone you had never seen before."

"I was too frightened to think of anything: but the face struck me as one I had never seen before."

"Was it the face of a woman?"

"Yes."

"And it had long white hair, I understand?

"Yes."

"Will you swear it was not the face of Mrs. Armstrong?"

"I don't know."

"In point of fact you will admit that it might have been her face?"

"It might have been, but it turned away so quickly that I had hardly time to—"

"Quite . . . you had not time to recognise it: but the expression of hatred was so obvious that you recognised that at once."

"Yes."

"Thank you. How long after this was it that you saw Mrs. Armstrong?"

"We went straight into the house and into the drawing-room. Mrs. Armstrong joined us there in a few minutes."

"How many minutes?"

"Only two or three."

"Did you mention having seen the face?"

"Oh yes. I pointed it out to Robert at once, and afterwards to his mother in his presence . . . afterwards, as you know, to Mary the cook."

'What view did Robert Armstrong take?"

"He laughed at me and offered to go up to his laboratory and prove there was no one there."

"He said you were dreaming in fact?"

"Yes."

"And did his mother say the same thing?"

"Yes. She said there could not be anyone up there."

"Did this assurance dispel your fears?"

"Oh no. I still felt frightened, and I spent the night in the room of Robert's sister Kathleen."

"The plump young woman with the bobbed hair?"

"Oh yes."

"And you slept well in her company?"

"Yes—although I was some time actually going to sleep."

"And you heard nothing?"

"No."

"Had you any reason to doubt that either Robert Armstrong or his mother or both really believed that you only imagined that this face had looked down upon you from the laboratory window?"

"I don't quite understand."

"What I mean is this"—said the detective—"when you told them of what you had seen how did they take it—which did you tell first? The young man, I suppose?"

"Yes."

"Well—how did he take it?"

"He just laughed at me for being so fanciful."

"You are sure that there was nothing in his manner to suggest that he knew there might be somebody—his mother for instance—watching from his laboratory?"

Dora hesitated for ever such an instant and then said,

"Quite sure."

It was the nearest approach to a falsehood she had ever uttered in her life.

"I see. And what about Mrs. Armstrong? Did she suggest in her manner that she thought you had seen too much?"

"No."

Dora had withheld information as to the real impression she had received of the way Mrs. Armstrong and Robert took her vision of the face at the window, because she wished at all costs to try to destroy that impression in the detective's mind planted there she felt sure by the gardener and Mary, that Mrs. Armstrong and her son could have quarrelled severely over his engagement to her. Such an impression was certain to involve Robert in the murder.

But Bradfield was far too old a bird to be altogether deceived by so simple an artifice. He could see clearly that the girl was terribly embarrassed as she uttered the last two replies, and gauged her character with very creditable accuracy. So he took her assurances with just the slightest pinch of salt, and dropped this particular part of his examination for the moment, hoping to glean some more information later on.

"Tell me now, in confidence, Miss Owen," said he, "what are Robert Armstrong's financial prospects?"

"I don't know."

"But as his fiancée, surely you have some idea as to his means? What does he do for a living—does he hold any appointment?"

"Oh no. He is a man of private means."

"His science is purely his hobby?"

"I believe so."

"Do you know where these private means of his come from?"

"No."

"Are they entirely independent of his mother or his father's means?"

"I think so."

"Are you sure?"

"Well—not quite sure, but to the best of my belief his money does not come from either of his parents. Why ask me—why not ask Robert himself?"

"I'm going to—later," said Bradfield. "In the meantime I should just like to know one thing—and you must forgive me asking you such an entirely personal question but it is my duty and I have no choice. Has Robert Armstrong entangled himself with you in any way which would make it imperative for him to have offered you marriage?"

"Most certainly not. He is the last man on earth to do such a thing."

There was such a ring of sincerity in her reply and such a tone of righteous wrath that Bradfield believed her, and apologised for asking such a question.

"We are coming right down to brass tacks now, Miss Owen," said he—"right down to this very night. What time did you go to bed?"

"About eleven."

"You slept in your own room?"

"Yes."

"Did you hear any noise or disturbance in the night?"

Dora felt terrible. Now she must deliberately begin to lie. The detective must not know of what took place in her room. She pulled herself together, gripped the arm of a chair in which she was sitting, and replied,

"I have never slept better in my life. The moment my head touched the pillow I was asleep and I was roused up from my bed by your own constable with the news that this dreadful thing had happened in the night."

"Humph!" muttered the detective. "You must be a very sound sleeper. Your room, I understand, is next door to the one in which the crime took place, and the victim screamed once if not twice in a way that would have wakened the dead. It was heard clearly by the gardener who stood outside the house in the garden. Sure you heard nothing?"

"Sure." The words came through quivering lips.

"And what time did you last see Mrs. Armstrong alive?"

"When I said good-night to her on going to bed."

"That was eleven o'clock?"

"Yes—just about eleven."

"Did she appear quite normal?"

"Yes—quite herself."

"Where did you leave her?"

"Sitting in the drawing-room reading the evening paper."

"Was she alone when you left her?"

"No, Robert was with her."

"Thank you. I think that will do, Miss Owen."

Greatly relieved, Dora rose and left the room. She had barely found herself in the drawing-room again when she saw Kathleen ushered into Bradfield's presence, tear stained and trembling.

Robert was sitting staring straight before him, deathly white, with hard, set features, and Dora would have given anything to have been alone with him so that she might renew her entreaties for him to throw light upon all that was so dark and terrible to her. But the two policemen on guard, to say nothing of the presence of the gardener, and the collapsed Mary stretched out on a sofa, made any conversation out of the question.

Kathleen had been under examination for a period of time which had seemed an eternity to Dora, but which was actually only about ten minutes, when the drawing-room door opened, and a policeman thrust his head into the room.

"Will Miss Dora Owen kindly step this way."

Dora felt herself turn deathly white, as, trembling in every limb, and with cold shivers of fear darting down her spine, she followed the constable across the hall into the dining-room.

Detective-Inspector Bradfield was seated at the table in the middle of the room upon which now were spread a number of small articles which had evidently been brought for examination by a second plain clothes man who stood by his side. Kathleen was huddled in an arm chair looking grey and drawn, mopping her red and swollen eyes with a handkerchief.

As Dora entered the room, Bradfield looked up from the note book before him and said very sternly:—

"You insisted, did you not, Miss Owen, that you heard no disturbance of any kind?"

Dora's mouth formed the word "Yes."

"I should be interested to know, then," continued the Detective coldly, "how you propose to reconcile this statement of yours with the evidence of Miss Kathleen Armstrong who tells me that her room is directly opposite your own: and that although an exceptionally heavy sleeper, she was aroused by repeated screams of terror which came from the direction of your bedroom and which she recognised as being in your own voice, which screams by the way came some minutes before the shriek made by the murdered woman which she also heard soon afterwards. Not only so, but examination of your room has brought to light the sheath belonging to the dagger with which the crime was committed, and several torn fragments from the dead woman's dress have been found by your bedside with certain other signs shewing very clearly that a violent struggle must have taken place within a foot of where you were lying, if, at the time, you were in bed."

CHAPTER VI

DORA REELED, and caught hold of the edge of the table to save herself from falling. What could she say?

She had been caught "red-handed" in the first real falsehood of her life, and what was worse the police knew of that furious struggle which had taken place in her room.

Kathleen—and possibly others—had heard it, and actual evidence in the shape of torn fragments of Mrs. Armstrong's dress had been found.

But it did not necessarily follow that Kathleen or anyone else had actually *seen* the tussle: nor, apparently, had any clue come to light which pointed to Robert having been involved.

So Dora decided that she had better "stick to her guns" and insist that whatever noise, struggle or confusion might have taken place it did not wake her—even though it had aroused other people in more distant parts of the house.

What else under the circumstances could she do? To confess that she had been aroused would mean to confess that she had *seen:* she would be asked to identify the second person, and even if she declared that she had not been able to recognise anyone concerned would not they refuse to believe one who had just confessed to having bourne false witness in the first instance. Obviously.

So she pulled herself together with an effort, and replied:—

"Whatever may have been found in my room, and whatever anybody may have heard, I can only repeat what I said before, Inspector—I saw nothing, and heard nothing of this crime."

The detective looked at her steadily for a moment, and Dora forced herself to look him in the eyes for an instant before averting her gaze.

Then, "you forget that screams were heard, and recognised for your screams, Miss Owen," he snapped.

"That must have been a mistake," replied Dora, "unless—that is—I screamed in my sleep at some bad dream I've forgotten all about."

Bradfield grunted angrily. 'So you insist upon your evidence being absolutely accurate?"

"Yes."

"And you are prepared to swear that you have told the truth, the whole truth, and nothing but the truth?"

"Yes."

"Very well. But, candidly, Miss Owen, I think that you are perjuring yourself pretty badly. I may, possibly, be wrong, of course—but we shall see."

He picked tip a fountain pen from the table.

"Kindly sign the transcript of your evidence."

With trembling fingers Dora wrote her name at the foot of the notes, and handed the pen back to Bradfield who turned to the constable nearby, saying,

"Conduct Miss Owen and Miss Armstrong back to the drawing-room, Collins, and bring in Robert Armstrong, the dead woman's son. It will be interesting to have his version of all this—he's our last witness until we can get hold of his father, isn't he?"

"Yessir."

Bradfield grunted, and dismissed the man with a wave of his hand, who led both Kathleen and the trembling Dora out of the room.

Two minutes later Robert Armstrong faced Detective-Inspector Bradfield across the oaken dining-table. Save that he was deathly pale, Robert's face was utterly expressionless, his eyes merely staring straight ahead like those of a waxwork. His mind, too, seemed to be far away, as if he were thinking very deeply about something or other entirely unconnected with the tragedy that had taken place in his home that night.

"You are Robert Armstrong?"

"Yes."

"The son of James Armstrong and his wife Clara Armstrong?"

"Yes."

"Age?"

"Thirty-three."

"Profession?"

"I am engaged in experimental science."

"Good. Now can you tell me where your father is just now?"

"I have not the least idea."

"Can you tell me when he is likely to return home?"

"No. Mother was the only person who knew where he went to."

"Does he make a practice of going away like this and not telling a soul where he is going?"

"Sometimes he makes no secret as to where he is going, and at others he will tell nobody except mother."

"Is he away on business?"

"I believe so."

"What business does he follow?"

"None at all."

"But you said he was away on business."

"He writes books on electricity, and goes away sometimes about them. He is an expert you see—but retired years ago."

"Well off, no doubt?"

"Oh yes."

"And you—do you depend upon experimental science for a living?"

"No. I have two hundred a year of my own."

"Indeed. Where do you get that from?"

"It was left me by an aunt who died when I was a child."

"Do you make much money by your experimental science?"

"Very little. It is entirely a hobby."

"An expensive one?"

"Fairly."

"You are engaged to Dora Owen?"

"Yes."

"When did this engagement start?"

"The night before last."

"Was your mother antagonistic towards Miss Owen or to your projected marriage?"

"No, certainly not."

"Are you aware that there is a general consensus of opinion among the local tradesmen and both your servants here that your mother strongly opposed your forthcoming wedding?"

"No. Still, in any case there is nothing to warrant it. It is mere idle gossip."

"Is it a fact that you and your mother were in the habit of creeping about the house together after everyone else had retired?"

"I frequently sit up all night in my laboratory. But I am always by myself."

"Your mother did not sit up with you very frequently?"

"No."

"Did she ever do so?"

"She would visit my laboratory now and then when I was engaged in any work which interested her. But never late at night."

"Is it not a fact that on the night of your engagement, your fiancée saw a woman's face gazing out from the laboratory window?"

"It must have been her imagination."

"Must it? Could there not have been a woman up in that room then?"

"No. The room was locked."

"Miss Owen declares that she was not mistaken. Not only so, but others have seen some woman or other in that room by night at various times."

"I am the only living soul that has ever been there by night."

"You have never taken anybody up there by night—Miss Owen for instance?"

"Never."

"Now, Mr. Armstrong, I would very much like to know when it was you last saw your mother alive."

"I bid her good night at eleven thirty, and went upstairs to my room."

"You left her—where?"

"In the drawing-room."

"Alone?"

"Yes."

"What was the first you heard of this tragedy?"

"When the police called me down from my room."

"You heard no screaming or commotion?

"No. I heard nothing."

"I see. Can you suggest any explanation of your mother's end?"

There was a rather strange expression in his eyes, when, after a second's hesitation, Robert answered shortly:

"None whatever."

"Was she on good terms with her husband?"

"They were an exceptionally devoted couple."

Bradfield grunted, and glanced through the notes he had before him. Then, looking Robert straight in the eyes, he said,

"I have been informed that the night before last—the night you became engaged to Dora Owen—you had a conversation in this room with your mother behind locked doors in the small hours of the morning. Is this so?"

"Yes."

"What was that conversation about?"

"Something entirely personal."

"Yes no doubt—but what?"

"Certain private matters which concern no one."

"Now look here, Mr. Armstrong," said Bradfield forcefully, "I am in sole charge here, and I insist that all my questions are properly answered. I am here to clear up a murder, and I tell you candidly that if you put any obstacle in my way it will go hard with you. Since the victim is your own mother, I should think that you would wish to do everything in your power to bring the criminal to book—unless, that is, you have something to conceal which might otherwise implicate you personally, in which case you may rest assured that by concealing anything you are only proclaiming your own guilt."

Bradfield had hardly finished speaking when Thorpe, the second plain-clothes man, entered the room, and handed the detective a paper who just nodded and glancing at the document placed it on the table before him. Then he turned his attention once more to Robert with the words,

"Now, Mr. Armstrong, will you be so good as to answer my question—what was that conversation about which yon had with your mother in this room the night before last?"

"We were discussing the possibility of my continuing to live here after my marriage to Miss Owen."

"Oh. And what conclusion did you come to finally?"

"That I should have a home of my own elsewhere."

"Because there was an antagonism in your mother's attitude to Miss Owen?"

"No—certainly not."

"Your mother did not try to dissuade you from your projected marriage?"

"She did not."

"And was this question of where you were to make your home the only thing you discussed?"

"Yes."

"To what, then, did the words 'poor boy,' 'terrible,' and 'death' refer?"

"My mother uttered no such words."

"And pray who suggested that these words were uttered by your *mother?*"

Robert was silent—significantly silent, and Bradfield picked up the paper handed him by Thorpe.

"Here," said he, "we have your mother's will—or rather most of it—you see that it has been torn across. It was found—as much of it as we have here now—in the dead woman's clothing. I suppose you can't produce the missing piece?"

Robert shook his head, and the detective continued,

"Luckily we have here as much as will serve to shew the provisions of the will as they affect you"—and read out the following.

". . . I give and bequeath to my son, Robert, the whole of my property comprising the sum of twenty-five thousand pounds invested in War Loan—provided he either remains single during my lifetime, or marries only with my consent and approval."

After a tense silence the Inspector spoke again.

"The will is dated just twelve years ago, Mr. Armstrong— it must have been made upon your coming of age. It is quite illuminating."

"And so," gasped Robert at last, "you think I murdered my own mother."

"Never mind what I think—just answer me this question:—When and where did you lose that button which I see missing from the right-hand side of your dressing-gown, and which has seemingly been violently torn away by somebody?"

Robert put his hand, instinctively, to the spot where a mass of jagged threads showed that there had once been a button. At the same moment Bradfield held up the missing button and said,

"Here it is, Mr. Armstrong. It was found lying on the floor of Miss Owen's bedroom. Near it lay some fragments of the dead woman's dress. There was every sign too of a violent struggle—which struggle, by the way, did not arouse Miss Owen—or so she insists—in spite of the fact that it must have taken place within an inch of the spot where she lay asleep. But it did wake up your sister Kathleen who declares most solemnly that not only did she hear Miss Owen scream but actually recognised her voice as she cried out your Christian name. Further, she heard sounds which suggested that you dragged somebody from Miss Owen's room across the landing . . . I am afraid I must place you under arrest."

Of course, nobody realised more fully than Detective-Inspector Bradfield himself that the evidence against Robert Armstrong was purely circumstantial, and he anxiously awaited the report from the experts to whom he had sent the dagger with which the crime had been committed. But when at last it came it did not help him in the least. There were no finger-prints either upon its blade or its handle—the hand which wielded the knife must have been gloved. But if he could not strengthen the evidence against Robert, Bradford was equally unable to find any other likely victim. The whole household—with the exception of Kathleen—appeared to have lived the most retired of lives: to have gone nowhere: to have known nobody: to have no friends: and, most decidedly, no enemies. The place, too, was quite isolated; and its several acres of ground were surrounded by well-nigh unclimbable walls. Nor was there the faintest sign of anyone having entered, of having attempted to have entered, the premises from without on the night of the murder.

It seemed pretty obvious, in fact, that the guilty party must be looked for in "Restormal" itself—especially as the dagger had come from the wall of Dora's bedroom, where it had been hung as a curio: and, everything considered, Robert Armstrong seemed to be the most likely person: since, in addition to the clue of the torn button—not to mention the evidence gathered from the examination of other members of the household—he had a very powerful motive.

True, matricide is a very ugly word, and really Robert did not look as if he would hurt a fly: but the detective had little faith in human nature and none at all in appearances. So, in spite of his repeated declarations of innocence Robert was marched off to the police station to await trial for the murder of his mother.

He seemed quite resigned to his fate, only asking permission to bid Dora good-bye-which was, of course, granted.

Horrified at his arrest, the girl, nevertheless, steadfastly refused to believe her lover guilty—in spite of the fact that she had with her own eyes seen him dragging that midnight visitant from her room—evidence far more damning than anything the police had yet gleaned. But she felt absolutely certain that there must be some other explanation which would cover the facts.

Suicide, for instance.

Yes, that must be the key to the mystery. That woman who had crept into her room was Mrs. Armstrong: she had secretly hated Dora: and possibly her mind was a little unhinged. She must have crept into her room to murder her in her sleep, and Robert must have had some reason to suspect her, and watched over his future wife, caught her with that dagger in her hand ready to kill her victim, and dragged her from the room by main force, and Mrs. Armstrong, doubtleas, when she was caught red-handed by her own son in the very act of murdering the woman he loved, had a sudden revulsion of feeling, and committed suicide as result.

And now, of course, poor dear Robert was protecting his dead mother's name from scandal by withholding what he knew: was ready, in fact, to die on the scaffold as a matricide to avoid having to expose his mother's attempted murder of Dora Owen.

But when she propounded this theory to Bradfield, he was dubious—very dubious, and said that the wound in the dead woman's neck was in a position making self-infliction an improbability.

"But I know Robert is innocent . . . I know it," declared Dora passionately.

"Oh indeed? how do you *know?*"

"How could anyone help but know it? Robert would not harm a fly. I tell you he just could not be a murderer, and if you hang him, you'll be a murderer yourself."

Hard-boiled man as he was, Bradfield could not help but feel a trifle uncomfortable. It was only circumstantial evidence, after all.

"I am only trying to do my duty, Miss Owen," he said rather stiffly—in a tone, almost, as if he were arguing with himself—"and if there should be anybody wrongfully hanged it will be the judge and the jury that will be responsible."

"If any judge hangs Robert he'll be a criminal!"

"Nobody says he is going to be hanged—and judges are very careful when it comes to the death sentence."

"What's the good of your talking like that!" blazed Dora, "when you are taking him away to prison to charge him with murder: what do you care about his guilt or innocence as long as you find a victim in somebody who has no way of proving his innocence so that you can say that you have solved the mystery."

"Don't excite yourself, Miss Owen," replied the detective. "You will find that the law will not allow an innocent person to suffer."

"Have not scores of people been hanged who were really not guilty at all."

"A few perhaps, but a very very few."

"Very *few*!" gasped Dora, now beside herself with desperation. "If I had the power to make a law it should be that if a judge condemned anybody to death wrongfully he should himself be hanged when the truth came to light."

"You forget that the verdict is actually given by the jury and not by the judge."

"Then the jury should be hanged too. If they had the noose dangling over their heads during every trial they'd think twice before sending a man to his death."

But pleading, argument, and vituperation alike were useless. Two minutes later Dora had flung herself upon her knees beside the drawing-room sofa sobbing her broken heart out.

They had taken Robert away!

They say that "it never rains but it pours," and there seems often to be very considerable justification for the survival of the phrase. Just as good fortune is apt to be followed by good fortune, so tragedy frequently is succeeded by tragedy.

It was so in the present instance. Hardly had Bradfield taken Robert Armstrong from that stricken house to face a probable charge of murder—murder, too, of his own mother: hardly had the household recovered from the first dreadful shock of this unspeakably horrible crime, when there came to "Restormal" a telephone message from the provinces.

A man who had been staying for some days at an hotel in Birmingham had been discovered shot through the heart early that morning.

And the name of that man was James Armstrong—the husband of the woman for the murder of whom Detective-Inspector Bradfield had arrested the son of the house.

CHAPTER VII

WHEN DETECTIVE-INSPECTOR BRADFIELD was informed of the second tragedy which had fallen upon "Restormal" household, the immediate effect of the news was to send his theory of the case to pieces.

Up to now he had regarded the affair as a semi-accidental crime: the outcome of a passionate quarrel between Robert and his mother regarding Dora Owen. The suggestion Dora had made that Mrs. Armstrong had entered her room to do her some injury—possibly to murder her—tended, of course, to confirm this impression, and although he took the girl's idea that Mrs. Armstrong had committed suicide because she was caught in the act by Robert, with a distinct "pinch of salt," Bradfield filed away the possibility in his mind for future reference.

Still, he thoroughly believed that it had been Robert's hand which had struck the fatal blow, and felt convinced that any jury would agree with him. He considered, in fact, that Robert's one chance of escaping the death-penalty lay in the possibility that he might be able to establish that the stabbing took place in the dark and as an act of self-defence. But in view of the tale told by the gardener and the cook of the lights in that establishment being continually on all night, together with the fact that there were two policemen who could swear to having found the whole house illuminated at the unearthly hour when they had been summoned by the gardener and discovered the murder, made the hope a very slender one.

But what about the death of James Armstrong—Robert's father—in Birmingham? He must have died within an hour or two of his wife: possibly, at the same moment. Was it just a coincidence or was there scone connecting link between the two tragedies? If the latter, might it not point to the possibility of Robert's story of his being innocent of his mother's death being true? Might not both Mr. and Mrs. Armstrong be the victims of a gang?—but for the distance by which they were separated and the close proximity of the times the deaths occurred it would look as if the murders were the work of one assassin.

Then again, was James Armstrong's death murder or suicide, or could it possibly have been an accident? And if suicide, could the suicide have anything to do with the strange happenings at "Restormal" which had culminated in Mrs. Armstrong's terrible end? What did James Armstrong know of those midnight visits of his wife to Robert's laboratory— was there any possibility that he could have foreseen the tragedy of the bloodstained dagger which had fallen upon his home in his absence? And what actually had been the purpose of his visit to Birmingham?

But might not the thing be entirely a coincidence, and there be no connection whatsoever between the death of James Armstrong and that of his wife.

The whole thing was a puzzle, and, try as he would, Bradfield could come to no satisfactory conclusion. So, leaving Robert under lock and key, he took a personal trip to Birmingham where he saw his provincial colleagues who had charge of the case, made all the enquiries he could, and attended the inquest. It appeared that James Armstrong had been locked in his room in the hotel when the shot was fired, and as this room was on the third floor, and the revolver Mr. Armstrong's own weapon licenced to him by the Metropolitan Police and had been found gripped in his dead hand, the Coroner's jury brought in a verdict of "suicide while of unsound mind,"—the Birmingham Police Inspector, who had been seen by Bradfield, taking the view that the happenings at "Restormal" could have had no connection whatever with the death of James Armstrong.

So the morning following the inquest, the body was duly granted a burial certificate, and sent home for a funeral. But Bradfield returned to London feeling anything but convinced in his mind that there was not something more in the matter than met the eye, and so, although a trifle startled, was not altogether surprised to find upon his return to the Yard that there was an urgent message for him requesting his immediate presence at "Restormal," where it seemed something extraordinary had occurred during the night.

Seagar the gardener declared that he had seen a light in Robert's deserted laboratory, and, silhouetted against the window, the outline of the same woman whom he had seen before, and who was, he declared, none other than the dead Mrs. Armstrong. His testimony, moreover, was supported both by Mary the cook—who was in a state of collapse through sheer terror—and by Dora Owen.

If one wants to be rid of those followers euphemistically known as "friends," and of those even worse human appendages designated "relatives," it is only necessary suddenly to make it known that one is under a cloud and that the police are "in possession"; and even the free application of Keating's powder coupled with fumigation could hardly be more effective. Next to poverty, trouble is one of the finest known expungers of vermin.

Thus had Mr. and Mrs. Armstrong died natural deaths, it is beyond question that—in view of their very ample means—"Restormal" would pretty soon have been flooded out with aunts, uncles, cousins, nephews and nieces, pals, friends, neighbours and acquaintances, known and unknown from every quarter of the globe, complete with mourning attire and wreaths of every size and shape all ready to "do anything in their power to help"—since there was little danger of being asked to contribute to the funeral expenses.

But, as things turned out, such sympathetic souls made themselves very scarce indeed. A suicide is a very unpleasant thing—and when it is thought that a woman has been murdered by her own son no self-respecting friend of either party would dream of being involved in such a disgraceful scandal. Not that there was any question of narrow-mindedness though—no one would have quarreled in the least with exactly *how* the Armstrongs came to die, provided the will was satisfactory and there could be no publicity. But since it seemed that Robert had been "found out," and the thing would soon be in all the papers, well, naturally enough, all and sundry were careful to keep themselves well in the background until the clouds had lifted, all forms of law complied with, all legal costs paid, and the provisions of the will made known, when they could safely come carefully forward and collect anything to which they might be entitled or to which they could without personal risk formulate any sort of claim-lawful or otherwise.

So since it seemed to Dora Owen that the Armstrongs had no friends and no relations at all, she took the rather unusual view that it was her duty to stay at "Restormal" and see everything through to the bitter end, in spite of the fact that she was almost certain that her name did not receive favourable mention in either Mr. Armstrong's will or that of his wife. And, indeed, her presence there was somewhat pressingly necessary since poor Kathleen had collapsed and been taken to a nursing-home and so—after Mrs. Armstrong's body had been carried off to the mortuary—the place was quite empty save for Mary the cook who was nothing more than a nervous wreck—and Seagar, the gardener, whose plight was but little better: both of whom, by the way, would have lost their jobs had not Dora kept them on.

But it wanted no little courage to stay in that great desolate house at whose door grim death had knocked twice within twenty-four hours, leaving behind him the shadow of his dreadful ministers Murder and Suicide.

Had Dora been a differently constituted girl there can be little doubt that she would have left "Restormal" immediately after Robert's arrest and taken refuge in the quiet little country village of which her father was the vicar. But she was one of those women who are faithful to the death, and so she made up her mind that at any cost she would see everything through to the bitter end if only for Robert's sake.

Although her anxiety as to her lover's fate was beyond description, she never entertained for one moment a trace of doubt as to his innocence, and so deep and unshakable was her faith in his character that she determined that even if the Courts should prove him guilty she would never accept their verdict as being anything more than a blunder born of circumstantial evidence. But she also made up her mind that at all costs Robert must be acquitted, and, as the door closed on her lover's departure with the police, Dora vowed that every penny she possessed in the world should, if need be, be expended in the hiring of a Counsel second to none for putting up unanswerable arguments: one able when required even to prove that black is white or that human nature in general is tolerably decent.

Such a man would certainly be able to defend Robert successfully if it were not quite beyond mortal power to snatch the victim of circumstantial evidence out of the clutches of the law.

It was not more than an hour after Robert's arrest that the mortal remains of poor Mrs. Armstrong were removed from the house for the post-mortem examination at the mortuary and Dora, who had never before seen a dead body, could not suppress a sick shudder as the swathed up form passed her in the hall. Brave girl as she was, she had not been able to face the ordeal of viewing the corpse uncovered any more than had anyone else m the household except Robert himself and the gardener, who had seen the dreadful sight before anybody.

This over, there was the equally grim business of Mr. Armstrong's homecoming to be faced: and as luck would have it the body did not arrive until fairly late at night which if possible added to the horror of the thing. The room in which the murdered woman had been found had been locked up by the police, and so he was laid on the bed in Robert's room to await the funeral—arrangements for which Dora had made earlier in the day.

When at last the men were out of the house, Dora felt too utterly worn out both in body and in mind to do anything more than throw herself on the drawing-room couch where she determined to spend the night. Not for any consideration would she sleep in her own room next to the place where Mrs. Armstrong had been killed and opposite the other dreadful apartment where lay the body of the suicide.

But, try as she might, Dora could not sleep, in spite of her utter weariness, and the luxurious comfort of the sofa, which was twice as large, and six times as soft as any leather-bed. She could only turn and twist and long for the unconsciousness she was denied, listening the while to the hundred and one little sounds with which the deadly stillness of the great house was simply riddled: sounds which seemed as if they were born out of that oppressive silence which one can *hear,* and that thick darkness which can be *felt.*

There was the slow, heavy, tick, tick, tick, of the grandfather clock in the hall: the muffled crunch of a mouse behind the skirting: the sudden scuttle of a rat as it dashed across the rafters above the ceiling. There was that mysterious creaking of floorboards and furniture so common in old houses, and that strange, dismal rustle of the ivy as it was blown against the windows by the midnight breeze: while, in the distance, came the dull thud, thud, thud, of some cupboard door which had been left open, mingled with the faint howling and baying of a tied-up dog as it struggled to free itself, amid the rattle and scraping of a heavy chain.

It seemed an eternity to the girl lying huddled up on that couch, before, at last, she found her eyes closing. But even then it was only to doze off for a few seconds and then wake up again with a start, aroused no doubt by the thud of that cupboard with the broken lock.

"Yes," thought Dora to herself, "it's that broken door that wakes me up every time and I could do with something to wrap round me—I'm cold."

She got up from the couch and put on the light. It was nearly three in the morning. Gracious, how tired and stiff she felt! No wonder either lying on that sofa instead of going to bed properly. Should she take her courage in both hands and go to her room?

No—the very idea of passing by the door of that room where the body of Mr. Armstrong lay in its coffin was enough—anything rather than that. Instead she would go to the kitchen and fasten that loose door, and get herself a coat from the hall stand. Then she could settle down again with hope of getting some sleep before morning.

Still, even to pass by the foot of the staircase leading up to the place of carnage, which had once been the best bedroom in the whole luxuriously appointed house, on her way to the kitchen, was a thing Dora did not relish over much, and it took quite an effort of will on her part to unlock the door of the drawing-room and leave its bright cheerful, snug atmosphere for the gloom of the oak-paneled hall.

She slipped out of the room, leaving the light burning, and managed after a few seconds' fumbling to find the switch which illuminated the hall. But either somebody had broken the lamp or the fuse had blown, for, when she put the switch on, nothing happened.

The hall light wouldn't work.

Dora hesitated. Dare she go alone all the way to the kitchen in the dark?

It would be a long, eerie, journey with a flight of stairs to descend too—and, even if she left the drawing-room door ajar, it wouldn't help matters much.

But what about that banging cupboard—really she ought to fasten it—she could never sleep with that thud, thud, thud, drumming in her ears.

Still, to go down to the kitchen in absolute darkness . . . with a corpse upstairs and not any living soul in the house beside herself (Seagar, of course slept over the garage outside, and Mary, refusing point-blank to spend the night in "'Restormal" in company with the dead, had defied convention with the privilege of her seventy odd years and slept in the room next the gardener.)

"Well, after all, what harm could a dead man do . . . why be a superstitious fool?" reasoned the girl's common sense.

Yet, rational as she undoubtedly was, Dora was only a woman after all. So again she hesitated before taking the plunge. She just could not make up her mind.

Then something happened which made it up for her: something which sent her back into the drawing-room and made her lock the door, put a chair against it, and leave every available light on till morning.

It came from the top of the house: out of the blackness of that great winding stairway which terminated just opposite the doorway in which she stood—a very distinct *creak* several times repeated—the kind of creak made by stealthy footsteps on a staircase.

Creak . . . creak . . . creak . . .

Dora listened intently. Surely her ears must be deceiving her. Why, there was nobody up there—not a soul—only Mr. Armstrong dead and lying in his shroud. It could only be her nerves.

But no—no—the sound again—and this time louder than before. Somebody was descending the rickety stairs leading from Robert's deserted chemical laboratory to the landing below . . . where in that room of tragedy lay . . .

Dora *felt* her hair rising.

Hark! What was that?

A moan—a faint sighing moan—caught her ears—once, twice, thrice, it was repeated.

Then it resolved itself into audible words, spoken in a high pitched, quivering wail,

"Help me, Rob! . . . Help me, Rob! . . ."

It was like the voice of a soul in hell.

Then again that dreadful creaking . . . this time . . . not the crack of a staircase, but the unmistakable groan of floorboards on the landing . . . and each creak sounded nearer *that room.*

God above! Could *something* be going into *him*? Something from that room of mystery under the slates: something which cried thus in suppressed torment?

Dora tried to move, but her nerves were paralysed with *fear:* she could not stir: nor could she take her starting eyeballs from the staircase which fascinated her as if it had suddenly become a rattlesnake.

And then, as her palsied muscles struggled impotently to regain the power of movement, the trembling girl heard that which brought her very heart into her mouth, and made the marrow of every bone in her body *crawl* with stark horror.

It was a tapping—a gentle insistent tapping on the panels of a door on the floor above: and all Dora's senses screamed aloud to her reeling brain which door it was.

Somebody was knocking at that door up there behind which the dead James Armstrong lay in his coffin.

CHAPTER VIII

WHAT WITH ONE THING AND ANOTHER, it was mid-afternoon before Bradfield arrived at "Restormal." He was met at the gate by Dora, and never, in the whole of his career, had the detective seen anybody so changed in so short a time.

Broken down by grief at her lover's arrest as she had been when Bradfield last left her it was nothing to her plight now. White, haggard, and trembling in every limb, her hair soaked with the cold sweat of fear, her eyes wide with terror protruding from their swollen, sleepless lids, she was strung to the point of hysteria. She grabbed Bradfield's arm convulsively the moment he crossed the threshold, and tried to say something. But so violently were her teeth chattering that it was long before she could utter articulate sounds.

But at last the tale came out, and Bradfield heard of all that had taken place in the night. Not only so, but the gasped-out account made him realise very fully how it came about that such a sensible, level-headed girl as Dora Owen should be so much affected.

And this was why.

She had not been the only person in the place to hear that terrible wailing voice. Both Seagar and Mary the cook had heard it too. Nay, more—they had both seen a light in the laboratory, and a figure silhouetted against the little dormer window—had watched it terrorstruck as it crossed the room to creep down those stairs to the body of Mr. Armstrong.

And they both declared that they had recognised the apparition as the dead woman—*whose corpse had been carried out of the house hours before darkness had fallen, by the police authorities.*

Small wonder poor Dora trembled and looked pale! Small wonder she refused point-blank to sleep another night in that house: or even to remain there after darkness had fallen.

It is bad enough to feel convinced that one has been the unwilling witness of something supernatural—particularly when the phenomenon takes place in a house where lies a dead body awaiting burial: but when, the following morning, one learns that one's frightening experience has been shared independently by two other people, and both these witnesses insist that they have *seen* something which we only *heard*, it is really enough to unbalance anybody.

But Detective-Inspector Bradfield did not believe in ghosts—or even in any life after death, and so Dora's tale failed to convince him that there was anything afoot out of the common course of things. He put down her experience to "sheer nerves" coupled with "the horrors" brought on by worry, sleeplessness, and shock.

As to the confirmation of her story by Mary the cook and the gardener, the C.I.D. man attributed the testimony of the former to "bad dreams" and that of the latter to an overdose of spirits of the variety which live in bottles during the earlier part of their career. True, their stories both tallied with one another, and with Dora's version, but then no doubt the three had conferred together and what the over-excited imagination of one did not furnish that of one of the others did. The whole thing must be nothing more than superstitious exaggeration of mere shadows.

Still, if Bradfield was a materialistic man, he was also an experienced criminal investigator: and so—especially in view of the various doubts he had in his mind about this curious case—he quietly—very quietly—determined to investigate that stairway and that ill-omened laboratory just to make certain there was nothing to be found out by Scotland Yard which might both account for the "Restormal" ghost story, and throw some new light on the tragedies which had overshadowed the place.

So, picking up Dora Owen bodily as if she had been a child, the burly detective carried her into the house, telling her that she had nothing whatever to fear from anyone living or dead, and that before daylight he would undertake to lay the spooks for ever—even if there were any to lay.

"If you really *did* hear any voice, Miss Owen," said he, "then depend upon it, it was a sound from a human throat."

"But it couldn't have done—I was the only person in the house. Seagar was sleeping over the garage and Mary insisted on occupying the other room where he has his meals."

"Then," said Bradfield, "you must have been hearing things, letting your imagination run away with you."

"But what about that shadow on the laboratory blind which Mary and Seagar saw?"

"That was imagination too, no doubt."

"I wish I could think so," shuddered Dora. "But I am absolutely *certain* I heard that voice—I shall never forget it to my dying day. And both Mary and Seagar say that they saw Mrs. Armstrong moving about in the laboratory."

"That is only their superstition. Mrs. Armstrong is as dead as mutton and is undergoing her post-mortem by now."

By this time they had reached the house, and Seagar hurried forward from the porch towards them. His usually ruddy face was as white as death and the C.I.D. man noticed that he was trembling from head to foot

"Thank God you've come, sir," he croaked. "There's all hell let loose in the place . . . she's up there . . . walking about in her shroud . . . I saw her last night . . . and I ain't touched a drop to drink for days . . . Mary saw it too . . . and it's done for 'er . . . she's been taken off to the hospital . . . nerves broken down. You won't leave, sir . . . not before I can get together my things and clear out . . . somewhere where *she* can't come . . . I can't stand it sir . . . I can't be near this place . . . it'll drive me mad, sir . . . mad . . .."

The man's state of mind was dreadful—his eyes were starting out of his head, and Bradfield saw in an instant that he was perfectly sober . . . there was no trace of alcoholism in his manner: only an awful fear . . .

"Look here, Seagar," said the detective, gently, but firmly, "are you sure that you saw someone last night up in the laboratory?"

"So help me, sir . . . I saw *her* . . . Mrs. Armstrong . . ."

"Where?"

"In that there lavatory up there—and there was a greenish 'orrible light up there too . . ."

"When did you see her?"

"In the night, sir."

"But how came you to leave your room in the night?"

"It was Mary the cook, sir. She wouldn't sleep in the 'ouse because the master's body 'ad been brought 'ome. She insisted on makin' 'erself a bed in the room next mine over the garage. About two, or, maybe, a little later, she knocked me up. She said she'd left somethin' on-—some electric fire or such and she'd better go and cut it off or it 'ud explode before mornin.' Said she dare not go alone and begged me to go with 'er. So I put on some clothes and soon as she was ready out we went. We were crossing the lawn when suddenly I felt Mary grab me by the arm. 'Look,' she gasps out—just as if she'd 'ave screamed only she was too frightened to make a sound. And look I did. There on the blind of the laboratory window I saw that there shadow . . . the same old shadow as I used to watch . . . before the missus was murdered . . . it was in a green, flickering fight . . . and it moved about . . . and, so help me, it was Mrs. Armstrong . . . and then Mary fainted right dead away and I carried 'er back to the garage and attended to 'er myself . . . I daren't go near that there 'ouse . . . And this mornin' when I told Miss Dora I 'eard that she'd *'eard* 'er voice—callin' out same as I did . . . wailing and carryin' on . . . 'eard 'er tryin' to get to 'er dead 'usband . . . It's grief wot's brought 'er back from the dead . . . grief it is . . . and she kep' on cryin' out ' 'Elp me Gawd.' . . . ' 'Elp me Gawd.'

Here was rather a remarkable thing, and its full significance was not lost upon Bradfield. It shewed that Seagar and Dora had really independently heard the voice in the night, and that they had not—as the detective at first supposed—

merely exchanged experiences in the morning. The gardener from outside the house had imagined the words uttered to be "Help me, God," when Dora, who had been indoors and so could catch them more accurately, declared they were "Help me, *Rob*." The gardener must really have heard the voice. Two people would not imagine identical—or nearly identical—words, and, if the tale of one depended upon what he had heard from the other, they would tally *exactly*.

"If you were not imagining things, Seagar," said he, when the old fellow stopped for breath, "all about it is that there must be somebody concealed in the house."

"It's Mrs. Armstrong, sir."

"It could *not* be Mrs. Armstrong, I tell you. There is no such thing as the supernatural. Is the telephone in working order?"

"Yessir, as far as I know."

"Good. I am going to send for some constables immediately, and we are going upstairs into this laboratory and watch all night . . . We'll lay the 'ghost' all right, and, if no ghost appears, we'll search the place first thing in the morning from cellar to garret. This may alter the whole aspect of the case."

He turned to Dora.

"When is the funeral to be?"

"You mean Mr. Armstrong?"

"Yes."

"To-morrow morning at ten—I tried to arrange it for to-day, but it was quite out of the question."

"You've done very well, indeed, Miss Owen, as it is. Have these people no relations or friends?"

"I don't think so."

"Humph. Tough on you. But I think that we are going to find out something important to-night—something which may clear Robert Armstrong—so you may thank the 'ghost' for that."

Dora was dubious. The idea that the strange happenings of the night were not supernatural at all but merely the manifestation of some living person was all very well in its way. It was far more rational, and, in the light of cold reason, much more likely to prove, ultimately, to be true, than any other explanation. But then, if so, it would mean that Robert had been concealing someone in his laboratory for a long time—in view of all that the gardener's investigations had brought to light—and that, if this person was really the murderer, Robert was deliberately taking the blame himself. And, finally, this person was evidently a woman.

Poor Dora! She would far sooner it had been a ghost—and even rather have believed Robert guilty of the murder of his own mother since if so it must be in *her* defence that he had done it.

But if it should turn out that he was shielding some other woman—

Still, perhaps, after all, Bradfield was wrong. But Dora was at bottom a sane, logical (as far that is as any woman can be logical) girl: and, now that there was a rational, strong man on the spot and the first dreadful horror was over, the materialistic explanation of the mystery did seem the more probable.

Dora was not the only person to whom this theory of the crime presented itself. Bradfield put two and two together in an instant, and made up his mind that before darkness fell he would get some enquiries put quickly forward as to the past history of Robert Armstrong as far as women were concerned.

Tactfully enough, he said nothing to Dora about his intentions in this direction, but got on the telephone, with the result that an hour or so later Scotland Yard was on the job, and at dusk when five policemen arrived at "Restormal" they brought with them rather startling information.

Robert Armstrong, it appeared, had been married to a certain Mabel Burne some six or seven years previously.

But Mabel Burne—or Mabel Armstrong as she then was —had died some twelve months before this story opened—died of heart failure and been buried in a nearby cemetery.

And enquiries made had shewn that beyond this single instance Robert had never associated with any women at all: had been noted, in fact, for his neglect of the fair sex

Further, all this information had been obtained from the most authentic of sources and by private investigation experts. Not only so, but, when asked to do so, Robert himself had confirmed the story in every particular.

But, for reasons of his own, Bradfield had been careful to give instructions that nothing was to be said to the prisoner as yet of the events at "Restormal."

"Still, there *must* be somebody concealed in the laboratory," thought Bradfield.

But who could it be? It was, to all reports, a woman who had been seen and heard: a woman, too, who must be pretty intimately associated with Robert Armstrong since she had been concealed in his laboratory and, further, since she had been heard to appeal to him by name—calling him "Rob," which, by the way, was a contraction of his name only used by one person—his mother.

And the only other woman—bar Dora Owen—with whom Robert had been intimately associated had been dead and buried for over a year.

Who then was it who had crept from the laboratory in the night—could it be that there were indeed more things in Heaven and earth than are dreamed of in human philosophy? Could it be possible that the spirit of the dead Mrs. Armstrong had been wandering about in the dead of night and had knocked at the door behind which lay the body of her husband.

The very idea made Bradfield shudder in spite of himself. What would that night bring forth?

But in spite of these new-born doubts which would creep into his mind, the detective forced himself to discount the supernatural entirely—at least officially—when he made his preparations for the search that evening.

Thus he had all the outer doors of the house both locked and guarded, and leaving the laboratory itself to the last, made an exhaustive search of every room in the place—

sounding all the walls for sliding panels or other secret re-treats where anyone might be hidden. But the search only made it perfectly certain that with the exception of the dead James Armstrong in the bedroom the house was quite empty.

Bradfield had examined the body prior to the search and found it quite undisturbed, which discovery was comforting, since had the midnight visitant been a ghost the locked door would not have prevented its entering the room as it appar-ently desired.

It must have been someone mortal who wanted to get at that body. But why?

Possibly because, in spite of everything, there actually-was some connecting link between the murder of Mrs. Arm-strong and the alleged suicide of her husband.

And now time would make this clear, and, half sub-consciously, Bradfield did not re-lock the door as he left the room of death.

There remained only the laboratory to be searched. Here—if anywhere—was lurking their quarry, and in spite of his hard-boiled common sense, it must be confessed that De-tective-Inspector Bradfield felt little cold shivers creep down his spine when, late that night, in company with two armed constables, he put his foot on the first of the long winding flight of rickety stairs which led to that ill-omened, mysteri-ous top floor of the old house.

The weather for some time past had been hot and oppres-sive—a real St. Martin's summer, and to-night it seemed as if the dry, concentrated heat of weeks reached its zenith. The temperature of that creaking, broken stairway was all but un-bearable. It might have been full noon instead of nearly mid-night as Bradfield and his companions crept up that steep and dismal path.

Up . . . Up . . . Up. The journey seemed endless. Flight af-ter flight they climbed only to find yet another staring them in the face—each older and worse kept than the last, and with the mildewed paper peeling in great strips from the sur-rounding walls and the filthy treads more and more rotten.

Up . . . Up . . . Up . . .The stairs had come to an end at last to be replaced by a corkscrew-shaped iron ladder with perforated steps taking them right under the slates of "Restormal" to a neglected and all but taboo quarter of the old house—which the detective felt more and more certain with every step he took, held some unspeakably horrible secret.

They landed at last in the middle of a long, narrow corridor simply reeking with the indescribable smell of baked dust and dirt. It was lighted by a single carbon filament electric lamp which hung from a length of greyish frayed flex in a holder seemingly impregnated with verdigris, and threw a dull reddish glow half obscured by its glass being caked with grime upon the place beneath it. How long it had been burning it was impossible to say, but it must have been for a very considerable time; since the coverless controlling switch was so corroded that the slightest touch would obviously be enough to send the whole thing to pieces. Indeed, it was a miracle that contact continued to be made.

The wonder was, too, that the lamp itself had not long ago burned out: but, oddly enough, this obsolete relic had withstood a strain few, if any, modern "gasfilled" bulbs could have survived. It hung there in its terrible desolation like the phosphorescent ghost of some forgotten sentinel guarding a dead city: like a red, sleepless eye—bloodshot and luminous from the unceasing vigil of years: faithfully shedding upon that dismal passage such rays of light as it was able.

And what a place it was, too!

Stretching some ten or twelve feet right and left, the corridor was, at its loftiest point, barely high enough to enable a man to stand upright. It terminated at both ends in heavy fast-closed doors which looked as if they had not been touched for years. The floor was covered with loose, rotting boards without a trace of carpet or lino, and the crumbling ceiling sloped down on one side to within a few inches of the ground from a wall covered with black stains as if from the smoky vapour of foul oil lamps. Through a tiny skylight tropical heat beat down upon the heads of the intruders to

whom it seemed as if a lighted newspaper were being held in
their faces so stifling was the fetid atmosphere.

"Good Lord! What a temperature!" muttered Bradfield as
he set foot upon this eerie landing. "One can hardly breathe.
Who in the name of wonder could exist up here? Come on—
let's get it over. One of those doors must lead to the laboratory—if there is one."

He had hardly finished speaking when the silence of the
place was broken by a rumble of distant thunder.

"Hello!" gasped one of the policemen, "what was that?"

"A storm coming up," replied Bradfield. "Good thing
too—it will clear the air."

But there was very little conviction in his voice.

Suddenly the gloomy twilight was illuminated by a vivid
flash of lightning—followed immediately afterwards by a
prolonged crackling which soon resolved itself into a roll of
thunder.

"I thought so," said Bradfield, half to himself. "We're in
for it."

And they were, for the very next instant the storm broke
in real earnest. It seemed, too, to be right overhead—just the
other side of that frail skylight which threatened every second to break under the artillery of the beating rain which
without a moment's warning, poured down in torrents upon
its thin glass like hundreds of millions of tiny bullets: and
rattled against the surrounding slates like battalions of devils
hammering for admission. Rending the black canopy of the
heavens above, the lightning tore rough the heavy air in great
tongues of living flame playing threateningly on the roof of
that exposed house: the flashes alternating with deafening
claps of thunder while the wind screamed and howled and
whistled about the place with an abandoned fury which made
the constables fearful lest at any minute the whole edifice
should be torn from its very foundations.

For some seconds the three men stood stock still and
looked at each other. Deep down in their very heart of hearts
they all wanted to scuttle back whence they had come as
quickly as possible, but each would almost sooner have died

than have admitted it even to themselves. And it was really an unnerving situation to stand in that desolate place under the slates of a house of death on the track of what had been declared to be the spirit of a murdered woman with only the unbridled elements for company and having to trust to three very ordinary mundane revolvers for protection against something *they* knew not what.

"Come along," muttered Bradfield at last. "No use hanging about. If anyone is here they'll be in that laboratory—come on."

"Which is the right door?" asked one of the policemen, and the next moment he regretted having spoken for Bradfield gave a quick look round and said,

"I don't know—you'd better guard the one on the left while Bond and I investigate the other. The room may have two doors or there may be two rooms up here. Anyway we'll soon see."

Just for a moment, P.C. Taylor, to whom these words were addressed, felt a sudden terror grip his heart, and he was on the point of refusing outright to be left alone in that place of horror. But he checked himself in time, and, resigning to the inevitable, took up his stand as he had been instructed, while Bradfield and the second policeman went down the passage to the other door.

Perhaps never before in the whole of his professional career had Detective-Inspector Bradfield felt anything so akin to genuine fear as when he put his hand on the knob of that terrible door, whispering to his companion as he did so,

"Have your pistol ready—and prepare for—"

A violent peal of thunder drowned the rest of the sentence.

Plucking up every scrap of courage he could muster, the detective turned the handle, pushing the door deliberately inwards. It yielded, and swung wide open. As it did so, and the two men were about to step across the threshold of the room into which it led, there was a sudden blinding flash of lightning which for the moment froze them to the spot where they stood followed by a clatter of broken glass which was almost immediately lost in a clap of thunder.

The little dormer window in the laboratory had been broken.

By the time they realised this both Bradfield and the constable had entered the room, which was still in darkness.

Hardly had they done so, when, with a wild shriek, a gust of wind came whistling through the broken pane, and the door was slammed to with a sickening crash which in that desolate and terrifying place swamped even the barrage of the rolling thunder into insignificance.

It seemed to Bradfield that his heart had suddenly jumped into his mouth: and, forgetting that he had himself been holding that door when it banged, turned and angrily reprimanded the constable for letting it slip from his grasp.

Getting no reply to his irritated vituperation, Bradfield flashed his torch round to where he thought the policeman should be standing—only to find that his companion had slithered down onto the floor in a limp heap.

He was stone dead. The shock had stopped his heart.

Detective-Inspector Bradfield was alone on the wrong side of that door. What was worse, the ghastly discovery he had made gave him such a turn that he allowed his torch to fall from his hand, and, although he managed to recover it, it was useless.

Feverishly the horrified man fumbled for electric switches. Surely there must be some way of lighting this dreadful place! At last he found them: found, too, that they were only a mockery of assistance because they wouldn't work. The slamming of that door had sent that crazy carbon lamp on the landing to pieces, and, of course, blown the fuse.

There was only one thing to be done: he must find the knob of that door again, and get back to the landing—get Taylor's assistance at once. But he soon discovered, to his horror, that he had quite lost his sense of direction: that he could not remember if the door was in front of him, behind him, to his right or to his left.

And then, as he blundered about in that terrible darkness, madly trying to find his way back to the landing, he heard something which all but reduced him to a state of panic.

From somewhere out of that impenetrable night which surrounded him on every side, there came a high-pitched, quavering voice,

"Help me, Rob! . . . Help me, Rob!"

CHAPTER IX

POLICE-CONSTABLE TAYLOR WAS, perhaps, as rational a man as any other member of the force. But in spite of his common sense and level-headedness, he could not help feeling really frightened as he stood outside the door he had been told to guard and watched Bradfield open the laboratory, and when that terrific flash of lightning shattered the window and the door slammed to sending that solitary lamp crashing to the ground and leaving him in utter darkness, he was gripped immediately by a fear so great that he nearly lost his self-control.

"Inspector!" he shouted . . . Inspector!"

But his voice was drowned by the thunder.

Then came the comforting recollection that he had a torch in his tunic pocket. He found it, and pressing the button, sent a ray of light across the corridor to the laboratory door.

Bradfield and Bond evidently must have entered the room, as they were nowhere to be seen. No doubt they were exploring the place.

And, bit by bit, Taylor's self-control returned.

After all, this was only a job, like any other job. What was he doing, all said and done?—Just guarding a door in an old house while the Inspector hunted for some crook or other—and Taylor felt the friendly hilt of his loaded revolver with great satisfaction, and yawned—wishing that the said crook would appear and have done with it so he could get home to the sausages and fried onions he knew his wife was preparing for him.

Then, remembering that Bradfield had instructed him to be sure that he did not make his presence known, he switched off his torch and put it in his pocket again. That beam would give him away in no time.

But it was an eerie, horrible job waiting there alone in the darkness and listening to the storm: waiting for something to happen . . . It was a waking nightmare to poor Taylor—especially when he remembered that there was a dead body downstairs.

Then he remembered something else and he didn't like it a bit. He remembered exactly what Bradfield was investigating: that there were three sane people who declared that they had seen a dead woman moving about up in that laboratory: and heard her creep down those rickety stairs—after her body had been moved from the house.

Hist!—what was that?

Was it his imagination, or had he heard the door behind him open stealthily? . . .

It must be his imagination, of course.

Heavens, how hot it was to be sure! P.C. Taylor licked his dry lips, and thought lovingly of beer.

Two seconds later he felt something brush lightly by him.

That could not have been his imagination. Somebody must have actually passed him in the darkness: somebody must have come out of that door behind him.

He stiffened all over and listened intently—fearful lest the beating of his heart should betray his presence.

Yes—listen to that—creaking footsteps on those loose boards . . . and then—Oh horror—that muffled, ghastly, wailing cry,

"Help me, Rob! . . . Help me, Rob! . . ."

Then silence again. But Great God! what a silence: the kind of deathly stillness in which the panic-stricken "listen their fear" until their brains are turned and they become gibbering idiots!

Then again . . . muffled, stealthy, footsteps! . . .

There was a blinding flash of lightning, and, by its fitful glare, the terrified constable saw that his senses had, indeed, not been deceived.

A tall, thin woman with long white hair hanging round her shoulders, was slowly creeping down that winding iron stairway . . . her hands stretched straight before her as though feeling her way in the darkness, and her flowing snowy robe trailing behind her.

Almost at the same instant the laboratory door was opened suddenly, and Detective-Inspector Bradfield stood on the threshold gazing as if spellbound at the apparition as it slowly disappeared from sight.

The next thing that Taylor knew was that the Inspector was beside him, had seized him by the arm, and whispered,

"Down those stairs after her with me! Have your pistol ready: but not a sound for your life!"

Scarcely daring to breathe, the two men waited until the footsteps could no longer be heard. Then, inch by inch, they crept forward and descended those winding stairs in the wake of the white-clad midnight visitant.

Down flight after flight, the unnerving pursuit went on, Bradfield and Taylor keeping as great a distance as possible between themselves and their ghastly quarry who, thanks to this precaution, seemed quite unconscious she was being followed.

At last, after what seemed an eternity of creeping forward, inch by inch, step by step, through an inferno of outer darkness, with only those dragging footsteps and that hollow wailing voice to guide them, they found themselves standing at the head of the flight of stairs leading directly onto the first floor landing.

Here Bradfield placed a hand warningly on Taylor's shoulder as a sign that they were to proceed no further.

The carpeted landing beneath them was lighted by a heavily-shaded semi-indirect, electric fitting which threw a soft, warm, glow on the surrounding darkness, and upon the woman—who moved slowly and silently towards the room where lay the master of the house awaiting burial.

Now that he could see her properly, Bradfield felt a little shiver of fear go down his spine.

She was horribly like Mrs. Armstrong.

A second later and she had pushed open the door of that room containing the coffin and disappeared within.

Hardly had she done so when a violent clap of thunder shattered the deathly silence, and, as its echoes died away into the night, there came from the place of death beneath them, what was, perhaps, the most terrible sound they had ever heard.

It was the passionate sobbing of a brokenhearted woman: miserable enough to listen to in itself. But what made it so dreadful to the listeners—who realised now for the first time that they were alone in that great house—alone with the *dead*—was that it resolved itself into words:

"Oh! My darling . . . my darling! Oh! My darling *husband!*"

Strident with agony came the phrase through that peculiar stillness by which thunder is so often followed, to be mingled with the crackling of lightning, and then drowned in the rolling of the chariot-wheels of the storm-god: filling the very souls of the two men on that landing with a shuddering horror beyond description.

Could it be that the *dead* mourned the *dead!* Could it be that Dora Owen and the gardener had been right after all: that Clara Armstrong had come back from the great unknown—a disembodied spirit which haunted the body of her husband?

Again came that awful sobbing: louder and more agonised than before—tearing through the howl of the wind and the beating of the rain like the bitter weeping of the damned from an inferno of mental agony, to rise, finally, through a tortured crescendo to a positive scream of woe.

It died down to a muffled choking, and ceased for the space of a second.

Then came the climax . . . the deadly, dull, boom of a revolver . . . a sickening *thud* . . .

Bradfield, who, up to now, had been standing as if turned to stone, in the most awful, strained, silence of his existence, now seemed suddenly to come to life.

"You heard it?" he rapped to Taylor who nodded.

"Well, it's a damned mortal ghost that carries a gun—come on!"

Dragging Taylor after him, he rushed helter-skelter down the stairs into the room from whence had come the sobbing and the report of the firearm.

Never in the whole of their after-lives did either Detective-Inspector Bradfield or P.C. Taylor forget the dreadful spectacle presented by that bedroom.

The open coffin in which Mr. James Armstrong had been laid had been dragged from its trestles, and lay on its side on the floor, the body itself being clasped in the arms of a tall, emaciated woman who, collapsed into a twisted heap, had an ugly, angular, gunshot wound in her breast from the powder-blackened edges of which was oozing a thick stream of blood. Her long, white hair, through the matted tresses of which glowed her large, dark, fast-glazing eyes, straggled over her thin, pale face, and her cheek was pillowed against the shoulder of the dead man. A Smith and Wesson revolver lay beside her with its barrel still smoking.

It was no ghost: no midnight visitant from the grave: but a palpable, flesh and blood woman, falling to sleep for the last time, who lay at the detective's feet.

But who was she?

Bradfield rushed forward, and knelt beside her, with the idea, no doubt, of trying to save her. But it was useless: he could see at a glance that she was dying fast.

Even so, the question uppermost in the Inspector's mind was, "Would she live long enough to clear up the mystery he was investigating?" He was by no means a heartless man: but years of criminal practice had taught him that it was essential for the common good to get right to the very bottom of any case he had in hand.

"Who are you?" he asked sharply. And then, receiving no response from the woman's pale lips, he shook her a trifle roughly and tried again.

"Your name, woman—your name?"

He had to repeat the question three times before, at last, he saw her lips move feebly, and, bending right down to catch what she uttered, heard at last the words,

"I . . . *am* . . . *Clara Armstrong!"*

"Clara Armstrong! . . . This man's wife!" echoed Bradfield indicating the corpse of James Armstrong.

"Yes . . . Clara Armstrong!" came very faintly.

"But Robert Armstrong identified as his mother Clara Armstrong a woman who was found stabbed to death in this house only three nights ago."

Robert's name seemed to rouse the dying woman from the lethagy into which she was fast sinking.

"Where is . . . my son . . . Robert . . . bring him . . . to me . . . I'm . . . I'm . . . dying . . . bring him to me!"

"He is in prison waiting his trial for the murder of a woman he said was his mother."

An angry light blazed in the woman's glazing eyes.

"He didn't do it . . . you idiot . . . he didn't do it . . . he's shielding *me* . . . I . . . was . . . afraid he might, poor boy . . . *I killed her. . . I killed her, I tell* you . . . and I'd do it again . . . she—"

Mrs. Armstrong sank back exhausted, and Bradfield strained eagerly forward, almost forgetting, in his excitement, that she was on the point of death.

"Who was this woman you say you killed?" he asked, "tell me . . . who?"

But all he could get was,

"My son is innocent . . . By my hope of salvation, I swear it. He's innocent I tell you . . ."

"Yes, I *know* he is innocent," said Bradfield, "and he shall be released at once. But tell me—I must know for your son's good—*Who was that woman he identified as you?"*

"Yes . . . she *was* really very, very, like me . . ."

A long, strained silence in which the dying woman fought for breath.

"But tell me, tell me," insisted Bradfield anxiously, "who was she . . . *What was her name?"*

"Her name . . . her name . . . you want her name?"

"Yes . . . do you know her name?"

The fast-sinking woman smiled very gently as if mildly amused.

"Why, of course . . . she was—"

And Mrs. Armstrong fell limply back into Bradfield's arms, stone dead.

Detective-Inspector Bradfield's first thought when Mrs. Armstrong had told him her name had been that she was only raving in delirium. But a moment's reflection, and it was obvious to him that it really was Mrs. Clara Armstrong and no impostor who lay there.

For one thing, her interest in Robert, and her anger at his arrest bespoke the mother—and who but a sorrowing wife would hold a man's dead body in her arms as she clasped the dead James Armstrong to her icy breast?

Besides, the corpse of the woman who had been stabbed to death, and whose murder Bradfield was investigating, had been seen by no one who knew her for the purpose of identification except by Robert, whose word the police had taken confidently as to the identity of the body.

Evidently he had deliberately misled them, and he wanted the murdered woman, for some reason or other, to be mistaken for his mother—whom, it seemed, had actually been the guilty party—and who had apparently been hidden on that desolate top floor.

As to the gardener's words—"Mrs. Armstrong, by the Lord!"—uttered, when, with the two policemen he had called in, he had discovered the body, well, the man must have been mistaken, led astray by the close resemblance between the two women—and, no doubt, because he knew of no other elderly woman in the house other than its mistress.

And Bradfield remembered how not only were the two women both alike, but the unknown woman's long white hair—so like Mrs. Armstrong's—had been covering her face when she was first seen by Seagar.

Every lingering doubt, however, as to the true identity of the suicide was, ultimately, cleared up on the following day when she was recognised and sworn to, as *Mrs. Clara Armstrong*, by Dora Owen and James Seagar who, of course, could only be persuaded to re-enter "Restormal" with the very greatest difficulty.

But why had she committed suicide so suddenly?

It was quite evident that she had been hidden by Robert after she had committed the murder, and so knew nothing either of Robert's being himself accused of the crime or of her husband's suicide. She had crept down in the night, no doubt, because her son had arranged to get her out of the house to a safer place until everything had blown over, and beyond doubt, she had committed suicide from the shock of finding the body of her husband so unexpectedly in her son's bedroom in place of Robert himself.

But still, the principal mystery remained unsolved . . .

What lay behind it all? Who was the unknown woman: and how did she get into the house and above all, why had Mrs. Armstrong killed her?

"One person, and one person alone holds the key to this mystery," said Bradfield as he rose to his feet from the side of the dead Mrs. Armstrong, "and that is Robert himself. And, surely, now that the mother—to shield whom he has been willing, apparently, to go to the scaffold as a matricide—is dead, he has no further motive for concealing the truth. Let us hope that he will clear up the whole of this ghastly affair—if only for the sake of Dora Owen."

CHAPTER X

THE STATEMENT OF ROBERT ARMSTRONG, M.A., D.SC, LATE
OF "RESTORMAL," ESSEX.

On behalf of the Criminal Investigation Department, Detective-Inspector Bradfield has asked me to take the police entirely into my confidence, and furnish them with a full, detailed, explanation of the terrible events which have taken place at my former home "Restormal," Essex, in the course of the past few days; and, now that my dear mother has passed away, and I have no further object in concealing the whole truth, it is with the greatest relief that I unburden my soul of its grim, pitiful, secret.

The name of that woman found stabbed to death by the gardener, and identified by me as my mother, was Mabel Armstrong. She was my wife—the wife who was certified as dead over a year ago—and this statement will tell, in the fullest detail, exactly how a woman believed to be in her grave came to be killed that terrible night by the woman for whom she was afterwards mistaken by James Seagar, and with whom I deliberately caused her to be confused—taking advantage of the likeness which existed between them.

It is an extraordinary tale: one which many will disbelieve, while others, after reading it, may regard me as a person of unsound mind. It is, nevertheless, a statement of fact as I feel convinced the Inspector himself—if no one else—will appreciate, since he will find that its every detail dovetails accurately with what his investigations already have brought to light.

The murder committed by my mother—if indeed what she did can only be designated by so harsh a term—was nothing more nor less than an act of the noblest self-sacrifice on her part by which she actually rescued me from an unbelievably horrible situation which might well have shipwrecked my reason—and one, I feel convinced, in which no human being has ever found himself before, or will, I trust, find himself again. But to my story.

The first of the two ruling passions of my life which, indirectly, have brought about the whole of this grim and terrible business is my powerful bent for natural science, which in the earlier part of my life was so strongly developed that it made me an old man long before I was a young one by developing my mind much in advance of my body, and so giving me an unnatural desire for the society of the middle-aged at a period when I should normally have made friends in the schoolroom, and in later years leading me to prefer solitude to companionship of any kind.

The second vein in my make-up which has so strangely ruled my destiny, is, perhaps, less easy to describe.

It began far, far, back in my childhood—as early as I can remember: a strange thirst for affection: a yearning for sympathy; a desire to love and to be loved; which, of course, in the beginning of its inception should have found consummation in my mother, but which, strangely enough—particularly in the light of after events—did not. It is impossible to say why, but during the first conscious years of my childhood, I formed the impression that she was always more or less angry with me over something or other which either I had or had not done—and in particular when I expressed any unhappiness. Moreover, as my father traveled a lot at that time she was a great deal away from home, and so I was left only too often by myself or in the care of servants.

In my imagination I conceived the image of a tender and beautiful woman: a vague, shadowy being who came to me in my dreams: someone, I remember, who had long dark hair like my mother's: but who was never angry with me, who never misunderstood me: in whose comforting arms, and upon whose dream bosom, the pain of that bottled-up loneliness of soul which I felt at this early period of my life, even more acutely than in later years, would spend itself in a flood of tears: and in whose embrace I found the only peace of heart I then knew.

Often—how often—I would ask myself:—"Where is she? this visionary, tender, comforting, presence?" and used to dream that one day I should find her somewhere in the flesh waiting for me. Never shall I forget the glow of exaltation that warmed my heart when somebody told me quite casually that when I "grew up" I should meet and love some total stranger: an ideal woman predestined to be the queen of my life: created and made for me by the Almighty: and who would love me as no one else could love me: not even my own mother.

I heard in half-wondering delight that the concrete realisation of the shadow being I longed for so desperately actually was, even then, waiting for me: was, in very truth, my other half: and that we should, one day, kneel together before the altar in the presence of the God of Love, when she would vow never to leave my side, unless, or until, death should take her from me: and that, even then, I should find her, still loving me, beyond the veil when it was my turn to go.

I did not tell my informant that I had met her shadow—or was it her soul—in my dreams already. Indeed, I had never taken anyone whatever into my confidence. I could speak of my dream vision to no one save to my own heart, and through the years which followed I waited and hoped for the materialisation of her image: longing for my dream to fulfill itself in reality; and wondering, a trifle bitterly, Why it was necessary for me to "grow up" before anyone could love me.

No doubt a sub-conscious desire for manhood induced in this way made me age unusually quickly, quite as much as did my precocious taste for the study of science. Indeed, it is more than possible that it was this craving for maturity which, in the first instance, prompted my devotion to things scientific:—being, as they were, the very last interests likely to be associated with childhood.

Anyhow, by the time I was eighteen I had distinguished myself with an honours degree in Chemistry, Physics and Biology, and, in recognition of my budding eminence, I had been elected a member of a celebrated learned society and a reader of its library.

Thus, in early youth, I found myself in the company of nothing but elderly and middle-aged people: outwardly a self-contained, prematurely aged, emotionless, freak, but inwardly as lonely and miserable a creature as can be imagined, secretly obsessed by the desire to love and be loved, searching, ever searching, for an ideal where she was least likely to be found, and intellectually unfitted for the society of those among whom the mate I needed so badly should have been sought.

It was not surprising, therefore, that when Mabel Burne was appointed as librarian to the learned society to which I belonged, and where I spent more than half my time, I thought I saw in her the realisation of the dream-woman whose image I had cherished, for so many years, in my heart.

She was then some thirty-five or thirty-six years of age, well-made and good-looking, with fine, dark eyes and long, black hair: and I thought her the most beautiful thing I had ever seen. In more than one respect she closely resembled my mother in appearance, and, no doubt, this factor contributed in some degree to the attraction she had for me.

To cut a long story short we were married by special licence very quietly at a little suburban church when we had known each other exactly six weeks, and I can truly say that I embarked upon that marriage with the avowed determination of devoting myself heart and soul to that woman.

I centred all my thoughts upon her: loved her with all the pent-up adoration of a passionately affectionate nature which for years had found no outlet: defied her in my soul, and worshipped her as what I truly believed her to be, the long-waited Messiah of my life. In the unworldliness of what I can only describe as my platonic innocence, I thought that our wedding-day would be the beginning of a new era of deep and perfect happiness: of a great peace like to a living Nirvana: and in my inexperience of human nature imagined that it would mean as much to her as it did to me—imagined, in fact, poor fool, that she desired to be loved as much as I desired to love her.

Hans Anderson's "Little Mermaid," in fact, could not have been more sincere about it. She had told me that she loved me, and that had been sufficient for me. It convinced me that she must indeed be the realisation of my dreams; the yearned-for woman-soul who was created to love me, and whose love would draw me a step nearer to the divine.

There have been times since when, almost, I have regretted that I did not die in the supreme moment of my brief happiness when I knelt at the altar of that little church by the side of my bride, with her hand clasped in mine, and the perfume of the orange blossom in her hair stealing through my senses; as I listened, with throbbing pulses, to the inspired words,

"Those whom God hath joined together, let no man put asunder." Perhaps it would have been better if I had died. I should certainly never have known the dreadful pangs of disillusionment which were to shatter my golden dream before my marriage was a day old.

Fate did not even allow me the solace of an unshadowed honeymoon.

Would to Heaven my wife had deceived me, lied to me, kept up some pretence that would have saved me from the agony of realising the sordidness of the brutal truth which, ultimately, she thrust upon me. I cannot help thinking that it is better to live for ever in a fool's paradise than to writhe for ten years in a wise man's hell.

And the pity of the whole thing is that she never realised that there was anything amiss with her attitude.

Her singular coldness and reserve during our very brief courtship, most of which took place at odd moments, in the most unsympathetic atmosphere of the library where she was employed, I put down to nervousness, excessive coyness, and "maiden modesty" on her part;—believing that it would all vanish when we were in our own little home and she had my ring upon her finger.

How bitter then was the discovery that my wife had not one atom of affection in her nature as far as I were concerned: that she had married me more on account of the advice of a maternal government than from any inclination of her own: and that she regarded our marriage merely downright, deadly commercial, business proposition—whereby, in consideration of her cohabitation with me, together with her most conscientiously given services as "housekeeper," I was to keep her in accordance with the best traditions of how she had been brought up to consider a wife should be kept—and no more.

As to her personal regard for me, I soon discovered that I played a very bad second fiddle to her own relations: one of whom, she told me, one terrible day, had, actually, written the love-letters which I imagined had been penned by Mabel herself out of the fullness of her own heart, and upon which my soul had lived for weeks.

The fact that Mabel herself told me this—not in anger, mark you, but in casual, ordinary, conversation, as a plain matter of fact, and in proof of the said relation's literary attainments, did more than anything else to shew me the psychology of the woman I had married—particularly her comment on the way I received the information:—

"You *have* got weak eyes, Robert—*they're running again!"*

She was, at best, one of those people who, while desiring the good will and approbation of the world at large—provided, that is, they have to do nothing to gain this advantage that will interfere with their personal comfort—have no use for the concentrated devotion of an individual: and who, while enjoying, in some degree, the society of anybody and everybody, have no really deep love for any living soul. At worst she was a bankrupt, both of heart and of mind.

While, in some respects, singularly childish, she was, in others, remarkably sophisticated. Her childishness, while it frequently gave her a superficial sweetness of manner, took the form not only of an extremely poor intellect, but of an amazing lack of tact and of self-control, and her sophistication gave her an unusually keen insight into the meaner and baser side of human nature; made her gauge everyone by the lowest and worst standards, and attribute every action to the basest of motives. As her judgment, of course, depended entirely upon intuition, which she possessed in a large degree; and not upon reasoned thought, of which she was all but incapable, she was, naturally enough, frequently wrong in the opinions she formed. But not always.

In an attempt to understand her point of view, I would sometimes follow the powerful searchlight which she threw upon the minds and actions of those around me, and, while I found she had made many blunders, I realised, bitterly, that she was, only too often, more or less right, and, in this way, I discovered many phases of life and character to which I had hitherto been blind. I soon discovered a sordidness and insincerity in the natures even of those near and dear to me, and began to awake to a realisation of the grim fact that I had practically no real friend on earth: that those who pretended friendship or affection to my face, jeered at me, wronged me, or robbed me, when my back was turned.

I would rather not have known. I would sooner, a thousand times, suffer any material loss through misplaced confidence, than be alive to the bitter knowledge that people only cultivated my society for the sake of what they could get.

Mabel was an enthusiastic church-goer: and this, when I first knew her, led me to believe that she was a devout, even saintly, woman. I soon found, however, that she regarded church-going merely as a symbol of respectability, and looked upon religion itself as nothing more than a "matter of form." She was constantly urging me to take Orders—her reason being that she considered the clergy to be people of considerable social importance, and that to be married to one of them was the safest possible guarantee of that surface esteem she valued so highly among the narrow-minded, backbiting, mischief-making, tittle-tattle tea party, sordid, money loving, class of plebeian snobs from which she sprang, and upon whom her every interest in life was centred.

Her attitude towards religion, which I soon found to be by no means a unique one, did much towards shattering the spiritual side of my own nature, and, at last, I felt I could hardly enter a place of worship without a feeling of heart-sickness so intense that, finally, I kept away altogether.

Possibly, however, the worst feature of my unfortunate marriage was my wife's attitude towards myself. Though she was a faithful, and, according to her own unnatural code, a dutiful wife, and prided herself upon the way in which she ministered to my culinary needs, her cold-blooded loveless-ness was intolerable. In the whole of the ten years we spent together as man and wife I don't think she kissed me a dozen times. In fact, she seemed to have an aversion to being made love to: to dislike being so much as touched: and she decried my attempted caresses and endearments as the "half cracked" ravings of a madman. A thousand times I tried to arouse some sparks of a normal human love in her heart, and a thousand times I failed so dreadfully that at length I gave it up in despair. The only passions her nature held appeared to be her easily aroused furious anger at more or less imaginary slights; an intense fear of physical pain; and a land of savage, dog-in-the-manger jealousy.

Not that she had any cause for jealousy, though such pain-fully extenuating circumstances as mine might well have ex-cused—or even justified—infidelity on my part: and, had I been less quixotically moral, there can be little doubt but that the affair would never have reached its unbelievably horrible climax, and, even though I should, ecclesiastically speaking, have had a sin on my conscience, my soul would have been spared the burden it now carries. Had I sought elsewhere the love my wife denied me, no doubt she would have quickly discovered my lapse (for she was of an extraordinarily suspi-cious and mistrusting nature, and would unblushingly open other people's correspondence and listen outside doors) and would have left me on the spot. And then fate could never have tricked me into a deed of horror beyond description: into doing that which mortal man has never done before in the history of our modern civilisation—from the frightful consequences of which I was, ultimately, saved by my sadly-mourned mother.

It came about in this way,—

My laboratory had not been moved from "Restormal" after my marriage, because, in the first place, my wife objected to "poisons"—as she called my chemical reagents—being in the house we occupied, and, later on, when I realised exactly what manner of woman I had married, I was only too thankful for the excuse of my work to take me out of her society occasionally, although it was only by representing to Mabel that I looked to my experiments for *her* livelihood that I was enabled to frequent the place without creating eternal domestic brawls. As it was she could say nothing to my daily absenting myself from home as if to a place of business to return to her in the evenings, though, upon occasion, she would offensively declare that I ran her down behind her back to my mother—for whom she had a deeply-rooted dislike—while, in point of fact, I never mentioned her name to a soul.

In an attempt to forget my broken dreams I buried myself wholly in my scientific studies. Day by day I lengthened the hours I spent poring over my books and instruments, until finally, I all but lived at my experimental bench, thinking that here, at least, was something which could never fail me. I forced myself to care for nothing else in life, until, at last, my whole being was obsessed with one thing alone—a burning ambition to do great things as a scientist: to discover hitherto unheard of phenomena: to dazzle the learned world with the results of amazing researches: and to revolutionise the entire field of scientific knowledge.

Unlike most scientists I was not content merely to set myself to describe *process.* I determined that I would *reveal origin,* and, little thinking to what, eventually, it would lead me, I made up my mind to discover exactly what was that mysterious form of energy known, for want of a better name, as *electricity*, promising myself that, if I succeeded. I would next set myself to solve an even greater mystery.

I would give the World an answer to that great and terrible question—*what is life?*

For months and years I "laboured with the keys of science" to unlock the door which would lead into the heart of the greatest of nature's secrets, and, almost, I was on the point of despair when, suddenly, an idea struck me.

Here it is copied from my laboratory notebook.

Life and Electricity have much in common. They are both mysterious forms of energy: they can both be invoked by human power, although, in each case, such invocation is purely indirect. We do nothing more than just "turn on the tap"—we cannot create. We merely obey a natural instinct on the one hand, and scientifically discovered natural laws on the other.

All we *know* about it is that we have attracted life or electricity, as the case may be, to earth from the storehouse of the Creator: and this storehouse, for want of a better name, we call "space."

We know, also, that space is full of electricity: we see it flash from cloud to cloud when there is a storm: and we call it lightning.

Further, we know that, ever since the world begun, *lives* have been coming out of the great unknown, controlling, for good or ill, those fleshly machines called bodies—and then *going back whence they came—going back into space.*

Space, therefore, must be full of lives, the lives of those who have left this earth, and the lives of those yet to come here.

Suppose then that life and lightning—or life and electricity—are one and the same thing!

Suppose that when man invokes life, or when he invokes electricity, he is, actually, although he does not know it, attracting lightning: in the one case to operate a human body for some seventy odd years and then to return to space: in the other to run a machine, and then return, ultimately, to space again.

May not lightning—the most terrible manifestation of the power of an Almighty Creator—be the concentrated essence of *life:* awaiting incarnation or re-incarnation through the invocation of man;—the power engineer appointed by the Godhead. And may not man's industrial application of electricity—really only chained lightning—be nothing more nor less than his discovery of a way in which life may be made to operate his machines—his Robots?

Suppose the wheels of our World-industry to-day are being turned by the lives which were lived two thousand years ago?

It has long been known—scientifically proved—that electricity does actually exist in the living tissues of human and animal bodies: that a Galvanometer can be made to move by the smallest section of muscle or nerve: provided the experiment is made before the tissues are quite dead. Dead tissues do not contain electricity. It is, also, an established fact that if a current of electricity be passed through the muscles of a dead body, the muscles will contract in such a way as to resemble a return to life.

Further, the body of an animal or a human being, very closely resembles, in certain essentials, an electrical installation. In the animal and the man the animating medium is carried from the brain or source of power to the muscles it controls through *nerves* which are cords of animal tissue—very much like the electric wires which carry electricity from the source of electrical power to the machinery it runs.

Again, Electricity is the only form of energy that will convey sound from one side of the world to the other. We can work a machine or a vehicle by steam, for instance, but there can never be a steam wireless set—or any other kind of wireless set—that can do without electricity and yet convey human voices from pole to pole without connecting wires. We think that we are quite certain that the voice is actually carried electrically across the intervening continents: in fact we say that we know exactly how it is done.

But just how can we be *sure* that the voices we hear from our wireless loudspeakers are the voices we imagine them to be: may they not be the voices of the *dead* mocking us by repeating in England the words uttered by living people in America: may it not be electricity that speaks: may not electricity be indispensable for wireless telegraphy because electricity is life?

Finally, spiritualists tell us that at a séance, when we join hands, and a force is generated whereby tables are moved, and things made luminous, these phenomena are brought about by the invocation of the *dead*, while it has been said by scientists that they are due to the electricity in the bodies of the *living*—i.e. the sitters themselves.

How do we know which it is—it must be one or the other—and how do we know which is which: which is electricity and which is life?

Are we not forced to the conclusion that electricity may be life and life electricity?

I proved my theory. Would to God that I had not done so. My dear mother would have been alive to-day, and I should have been spared much. But of what use regretting the past? Let me rather hold it up as a warning to others.

After many days and nights of incessant toil: after failure upon failure: I succeeded in restoring a recently dead cat to life by supercharging its nervous system with electricity— just as if it were an accumulator.

Exultation! I could bring the dead to life—that is, provided the bodies were undamaged: provided they had no severe wound, and their vital parts not crushed.

If only I could apply my principle to human beings I should be the greatest physician the world had ever known. I would have the whole earth at my feet. Supreme power lay within my grasp!

If only I could have the opportunity of trying my experiment on a human being!

Three months later I *got* the opportunity: tragically, terribly—

My wife died suddenly of heart failure.

CHAPTER XI

THE STATEMENT OF ROBERT ARMSTRONG, M.A., D.SC.—
CONTINUED

MABEL'S DEATH CAME as so great a shock that, for the moment, my senses were paralysed. We had been married for just over ten years, and, although she had never truly been a wife to me in much else than in law, although I had simply regarded her as she seemed to wish to be regarded—as a housekeeper, although I had been away from home so much of late, and, thus, seen so little of her: although, even when I was at home, she had always appeared to seek anybody's society rather than my own, and would spend hours on end in the kitchen gossiping with the charwoman and leaving me to my own devices: although her whole nature had been such a bitter disappointment, and, during the whole of our association, she had never shewn the faintest trace of affection for me, but had broken my heart, starved my body, and I all but murdered my soul: yet her death sent such a wave of powerful emotion through me that it seemed as if the world had stopped: as if something, which had long slept within me, awoke and cried aloud with an agony that could not be stilled: as if the tears which welled up from my soul thawed my heart—long frozen through years of neglect—once again into life.

Everything was forgotten—everything, when I stood beside her open coffin and realised that I was a widower. All the misery I had undergone during the past years was swamped out of my recollection by the pain I felt at her death. It was not the body of the cold-blooded, middle-aged, housekeeper, who had never cared a straw for me, upon which I gazed: it was the form of the woman in whom I had once thought I saw the realisation of a now long-lost dream: the face of the woman I had loved: the features which, years ago, I had imagined to be the most beautiful on earth.

And then, as I kissed the cold, dead, lips—for the first time unresisting since I had thought them mine, and bid a last farewell to the wife for whose love I had longed so terribly and so vainly, there shot through my mind a ray of an almost terrible hope.

I remembered what, until now, the excess of my grief had made me forget—my discovery—the unbelievable power fate had placed into my hands. Suppose it would enable me to snatch Mabel from the jaws of death? Suppose I could bring her back?

Would she, out of gratitude for the life I had given her, dedicate it to me, content to forget all the world beside? Would she realise that, in spite of the fact that she had never loved me or wanted my love, I had—out of my devotion—reclaimed her from the grave, and allow herself to be wooed and won?

I determined, finally, to take the risk.

But it was quite one thing to make up my mind to experiment upon a body awaiting burial, and quite another to put it into execution. The funeral was to take place early the following morning and she would be screwed down within the hour.

If I were to remove her questions would be asked: and what answer could I make? If I told them what was in my mind I should be branded as a madman.

The thing must, at all costs, be kept strictly as a secret—at least until after it was an established fact that I had brought my dead wife to life.

I should have to wait, therefore, until after the coffin had been fastened down, unscrew it, remove Mabel, and take her somehow to my laboratory at "Restormal." I was alone in the house with my poor wife, and "Restormal," too, was absolutely deserted, since both my parents were away on the Continent holiday-making with Kathleen—as were Mary the cook and the gardener—and they would not return for over a week. So there would be no obstacle here provided I worked at night and could convey the body without being seen. But I should have to put something in the coffin to replace the body, to weigh exactly the same, and not in any way whatever arouse the least suspicion that the undertakers' work had been tampered with.

Could I do this successfully?

After much consideration I decided that the risk was far too great in removing the body before the funeral. I must allow her to be screwed down, allow her to be interred, and then, when night fell, exhume the coffin.

This was not nearly so difficult as it sounds, because nothing is really easier than to pull a coffin out of a newly-made grave without the necessity for any digging, and in such a way that to all outward seeming the grave is undisturbed.

It is necessary only to bore through the earth with a long gimlet, get it well screwed into the wood of the coffin, and then drag the latter through the loose earth to the surface. But it must be done *immediately* after the funeral or the earth sets hard and the method becomes impossible.

For many, many years this method of exhuming bodies recently buried was employed by the "Body Snatchers," or "resurrection men," as they were called, in the days before corpses for dissection could legally be obtained by medical students, and it was formerly the custom to watch every newly-made grave until the earth had become sufficiently hard to render removal of the coffin by the gimblet out of the question. Nowadays, of course, the stealing of bodies being no longer necessary, cemeteries are no longer so closely watched—the "body snatcher" being quite obsolete and well nigh forgotten all about.

Mabel was to be buried, too, in a spot most admirably adopted for the purpose of such a secret exhumation. Her grave was only just inside the railings of the cemetery, and these were easy to climb besides being right away from any main thoroughfare—in a spot which I knew very well would be absolutely deserted by night. Not only so, but the caretaker's lodge and the main entry-gates of the place were a good mile from the grave itself, and so there was not much risk of interruption.

Further, by allowing Mabel to be buried, I was overcoming part of another difficulty—the cartage of the body to "Restormal": the undertakers themselves would convey her more than two-thirds of the journey, and it would be much easier to transport a coffin than a body in a shroud without arousing suspicion.

I could do this last in my own car.

Finally, I actually had in my possession one of those very long, thin, gimlets used by the "resurrectionist" of old which I had picked up at a sale of curios many years ago, little thinking that I should ever put it to its own grim use.

"I am the resurrection and the life, saith the Lord . . ."

Hardly had the words ceased to ring in my ears: hardly, it seemed, had the passing bell stopped tolling, and the inexpressible sadness of the ceremony at the graveside fully permeated into my lonely heart: hardly had the few mourners left the stricken little house which I had tried so vainly to make a home: before I found myself in my laboratory at "Restormal," bending over a limp, white form which lay on my electro-chemical bench. I had done it!

God, but it had been horrible! I have never felt quite the same since. To stand there alone in the darkness and the silence with the white tombstones looming like ghosts through the night as if to reproach me for my violation of then pitiful sanctity: to have the strange odour of the damp, loose, earth in my nostrils, as, fearfully, I pierced through the new-turned soil with my rusty instrument: to feel, at last, the screw bite into the wood, and then, finally, to drag, with infinite labour, that heavy load to the surface, terrified lest, at any moment, I should be interrupted!

It was an experience the dreadful memory of which I shall carry to my death-bed.

I had not been seen. I had not been heard, although I had been forced to drag the coffin along the ground, so heavy was it: and then, after climbing over the railings, to tip it on one side and pull it carefully through the space between two of the bars, which, luckily for me, were set very wide apart. Horrors, what a creaking and a scraping it made—the mould-coated wood against the iron: and what an eternity it seemed to take to accomplish the task.

And now this part of the macabre business was safely over, the coffin had been got safely to my laboratory and broken open. I had carefully examined Mabel and found that her body was in perfect condition, and that my gimlet had not so much as touched her.

As she lay there so still, and so cold, I could not help but notice that the coarsening of her features, which had taken place during recent years, seemed now, to a considerable extent, to have left them, and, almost, I could have imagined that she was not a day older than when I had first met her. Her face, framed by its long black hair not one tress of which, strangely enough, had whitened or even greyed, might have been a mask of alabaster so smooth, and peaceful, and delicate, did it look. More than ever at that moment did Mabel resemble my mother as I remembered she had looked in my early childhood.

Tragedy of the World that we should be born but to die! And how little is the pity of it mitigated by promises of a future life at some indefinite time, and in some indefinite place! How often, I wonder, is it the believer on his or her death-bed, rather than the mourner condemned to wait his own turn, who is comforted by the words,

"I am the resurrection and the life . . ."

. . . the resurrection and the life . . . the resurrection and the life . . . the resurrection and the life. I found myself repeating the words in a whisper, over and over again. And, as I did so, they seemed, gradually, to take to themselves a new meaning.

No longer were they the vague, shadowy, promise of some far off Divine Presence: to be fulfilled in Eternity: they were the words of concrete knowledge: it was not a matter of faith, but the certainty of an exact science. I had given her body resurrection—drawn it from the tomb with my own hands—that I might, here and now, re-endow it with life.

And, even as the thought flashed across my mind, the little dormer window of my laboratory was illuminated with a vivid flash of lightning.

Lightning! Flash after flash of it, alternating with mighty peals of re-echoing thunder. Lightning—leaping from cloud to cloud, and rending the black heavens with its power. Lightning which I, alone, knew to be the concentrated essence of life, now, even now, tearing the veil from the very womb of creation that I who, alone among mortal men, had seen within, might triumph.

What more did I need for my great purpose?

I threw open the skylight, which was in the middle of the room, and hoisted a metal conductor, fitted at the top with a revolving mirror, that I might catch, and draw into the battery of giant Leyden-jars, with which I had covered the flat roof of the house, the living flames which crackled and tore through the ether. I then connected these mammoth reservoirs with the primary coil of a huge inductorium specially constructed to withstand unheard-of currents.

Now the current from an accumulator of, say, four volts, passed into the primary coil of an ordinary inductorium will yield at the dischargers something like 10,000 volts by electrical induction, and so I had only to "switch-on" my apparatus to *multiply the incalculable voltage of the lightning by two and a half to three thousand times.*

And it is this colossal discharge which I would pass through my wife's body, and which would re-animate it.

One thousandth of such a discharge would, of course, have torn the house from its very foundations, but for a secret apparatus I had devised to do away with such a danger. Nothing will induce me to reveal the principle of this part of my equipment—which I have since destroyed—lest some misguided, foolhardy scientist such as I, should seek to follow in my footsteps, and defy the laws of God.

I laid the body on a specially-constructed bench, fitted a metal cap to her head, and metal plates to her feet, connec-

ing these contacts to the dischargers of my tremendous induction coil.

Then, trembling all over with a terrible excitement, I
wound up a clockwork device which would, at the right time,
automatically switch-on my apparatus and send the concentrated lightning through the inductorium, and a discharge
having a voltage greater than has ever hitherto been dreamed
of, through the body, the arms of which were connected with
a machine automatically performing artificial respiration.

I had eighty seconds to wait for the supreme moment:
eighty awful seconds of the most dreadful suspense which
any human being could know. I closed my eyes and waited
in silent agony, listening to that slow, torturing tick, tick,
tick, of the clockwork switch, and mutely counting:

One . . . two . . . three . . . four . . . five . . . six . . . seven . . .

. . . seventy-eight . . . seventy-nine . . . *eighty.*

There was a tearing, crackling explosion, followed, an instant later, by a deafening, continuous roar: and I opened my
eyes to see Mabel's body and the bench on which she lay,
literally bathed in liquid fire.

She seemed to have become transparent—luminous—her
every nerve, vein, *and* artery, blazed with dazzling, pulsating
light, and made her look like a human network of incandes-
cent wires; while her muscles expanded and contracted in
convulsive jerks giving a horrible suggestion of a woman
being burned alive in a kind of slow blast furnace.

I had to endure the awful sight for full fifty seconds before the climax came: before, with a sudden jerk, she sat bolt
upright: and uttered one long, piercing scream which will
ring in my ears until I die.

Like a man possessed, I rushed forward, and at infinite
risk of my life, switched off the current with my bare hands,
and tore the metal cap from her head.

God, Oh God! Her hair—it had turned snow white! And
her skin had become shrunken and yellow, and her face old
and withered, all in an instant. But her eyes were open, and
her hands clutched convulsively at my coat, and held me in a

grip of iron, which, at first, frightened me, and then filled me with a great and terrible joy. I saw her breast heave unsteadily as her breath came and went in great gasps as of one fighting for air: and, as I listened to the beating of her heart, the tiny throbbing I heard seemed to swell into the victorious roll of a million drums of triumph.

She was alive! She was alive! *she was alive!*

Yes, I had succeeded in my dreadful enterprise. I had brought my dead wife to life, at the cost of her every remaining shred of physical beauty. But, had this been all, I should have considered the price a cheap one. But it was not.

If she had been unnatural in her normal life, she was ten times so now: a withered, glassy-eyed, mummy-like figure which seemed to be animated only by the very worst characteristics of her former life—without a trace of humanity to redeem her. She seemed, in fact, more like a human animal than a human being.

In the sudden wave of emotion which had passed through me at her death, I had imagined that, if I were to restore her to life, such an act of devotion might soften her towards me. But it did not. When, at last, I made her understand what had happened to her, she attributed it not to my love of her, but to my love of science, and broke out into savage vituperation because I had dared to use *her* body for my experiment—forgetting that its success had given her back her life. Not only so but she was jealous, furiously jealous, because, instead of mourning her death my life long to the exclusion from my mind of everything else, I had spared a thought for the science which had now restored her to the world. It was in this strain that she would rave incessantly—showing me that in this second life of hers she was little more than a maniac, and only now I remembered how I had often suspected her sanity before her death.

I was soon able to see that she hated me whole-heartedly, and, after a while, I began to fear, and almost to loathe, that dreadful human monster I had myself invoked. I could never for an instant forget that she was a resuscitated corpse, and it was not long before I almost forgot that I could ever have loved this living dead creature which I had deceived myself into imagining could ever love me; and then, as I gazed, sometimes, in horror at her clawing, yellow hands, her eyes full of soulless hate—as she gnashed her broken, yellow, misshapen teeth at me in her paroxysms of ungovernable fury at nothing, I cursed the science which had given me the evil knowledge to make my experiment such an accursed success.

Thus perished the last interest I had in life—my work.

Fool to tamper with forbidden things. Fool to defy the laws of Nature! Fool to oppose the laws of God!

I had thought that my success would place me in the very forefront of scientific investigators, but I realised almost at once that to tell any living soul of what I had done would be impossible. I could not bring myself to speak of it. My one hope was that she might die a second time, and that, somehow, I could replace her, to sleep at peace, in her grave once more.

I kept her in an attic which adjoined my laboratory, and forbade her to leave it without my permission, but it was a dreadful strain to keep her under control and prevent her being seen. But for the fact that she was cunning enough to realise that—especially in view of the change that had taken place in her appearance—no one would believe the tale she would have to tell, and so, if she were to escape, she would be quite destitute, if she were not locked up in a lunatic asylum, I doubt if I should have been able to control her at all.

As it was, she would slip away whenever my back was turned, and, generally after dark, wander about the house like a disembodied spirit, and it was not long before everyone in the household became aware that there was something queer about that laboratory of mine, and, one and all, they became terrified of a moment's darkness, with the result that the lights were kept blazing continuously from cellar to attic by night and by day—even a dark corner would inspire ungovernable terror, lest the shadow form, of which more than a glimpse had been caught, should be lurking there.

Later—when Mabel's silhouette was seen on the laboratory blind at night, when I was up there feeding her, or otherwise ministering to her needs—the resemblance to my mother, which she still bore, made it locally believed that my mother and I were mutually concerned in my chemical and physiological experiments, and so would spend hours together in the laboratory.

As an aid to keeping my terrible secret I encouraged this impression.

I had been reduced to the point of a nervous breakdown by the time this state of affairs had continued for a twelve-month, and it was now that Dora Owen came to "Restormal" as my mother's guest: now, when I looked her full in the eyes for the first time, I realised that, at last, I had met the woman of my dreams—too late.

Day by day, hour by hour, I fell ever more and more deeply in love with this beautiful, warm-hearted girl. By the time she had been in the place a fortnight I knew that I could not live without her, and when I discovered that she reciprocated my feelings: that I had only to say the word and she would become my own beloved wife: the storm of conflicting emotions well-nigh tore my soul in twain.

The gates of Paradise had opened for me—and I had deliberately locked myself in hell. Salvation had come too late.

But was it too late? Could I consider that half-demented thing hidden in the room adjoining my laboratory as my lawful wedded wife, when our marriage had been terminated by death a year ago: when it would be difficult, if not impossible, to make anybody believe that she was anything more than dead and buried. What law could compel fidelity to one legally deceased.

Still, whether credible to the world at large or not, the fact remained that I had, voluntarily, and deliberately, restored her to life, and so, ought not I to abide by my own decision?

But stay—in reanimating her as I did, had I not, spiritually, if not physically, failed in my purpose. Mabel, as she was at the moment I speak of, could hardly be regarded as a

human being: and was it not enough that I had not only remained faithful to her in her normal lifetime in spite of circumstances which nine out of ten men would have regarded
as tantamount to a dissolution of the marriage contract, but,
in spite of everything, even gone so far as to give my wife—
who had really been no wife at all—a post-mortem chance of
making amends for all the misery she had caused me?

Surely now that my last effort on her behalf had failed so
terribly, my moral responsibility ceased?

If the knowledge that I had brought her to life could not
awake a spark of affection—nothing ever could.

Surely then, I was free to try again. Has not every man the
right to the love and possession of one woman?

But what about Mabel—what could I do with her—if I
should be lucky enough to win Dora Owen, the first essential
would be to get right away from "Restormal" to a little home
of our own, and then who would tend the hidden maniac up
in that attic—who would control her as I had controlled her
for twelve terrible months? How could I account for her
presence? If I told the truth everyone would think me insane—Dora herself included. And to take that hideous living
death to my home—even if it were possible—would be un-
thinkable: would be inviting disaster and giving hospitality
to a figment of hell.

After many days and nights of mental torture: of solitary,
agonised thinking, I came, at last, to a conclusion.

There was only one thing to be done and I must do it.

I must take a great risk, and make one last, desperate bid
for life.

*I must send Mabel back whence I had brought her—send
her back to the grave—kill her in cold blood and bury her
somewhere.*

I knew perfectly well that, if I were discovered, or if her
body were to be found, I should be hanged for the murder of
"some person unknown," but, even so, it would be better
than to leave things as they stood and go eventually to the
madhouse whither I realised, only too well, I was heading
fast.

But, even if it were never discovered, could I rest in peace with the knowledge in my soul that I had committed what was tantamount to murder?

Would it not only be exchanging one hell for another?

Here my powers of self-examination came to a full stop. I could find no answer to the question however I plumbed the innermost chambers of my soul.

Ultimately I was compelled—to save my reason from shipwreck—to confide the whole dreadful secret to the one person on earth whom I felt that I could trust—my mother.

It was a long time before she would believe that I was not suffering from some dreadful delusion. In the end, however, I convinced her that the tale I told was strictly, damnably, true, and, inexpressibly shocked as she was, she took the view that I was far more sinned against than sinning, and confirmed me in my opinion that there was only one way out—to destroy the monster I had raised before she could destroy me.

"You must remember, Robert," said my mother, when I told her that I feared that if I were to destroy that dreadful creature which had once been—in law—my wedded wife, I should never find peace of soul again—"you must remember that murder, actual murder, is the destruction of life endowed by God. In this case you will be doing no more than taking the life which you, yourself, gave. You would commit a far greater sin by allowing things to stand as they are—think—if she escaped . . ."

She was right. I had not looked on it that way before.

But it was one thing to decide upon such a course of action, and quite another to carry it out. Quite apart from my shrinking from the cold-blooded destruction of something which I had once loved, how was it to be done—especially in a house full of people! Whichever method I chose discovery would be almost certain.

I must wait until—in a month's time—my parents, together with my sister Kathleen and the two resident servants, went away for their annual holiday, and I had the place to myself. Then I could do it: then there would be a reasonable chance of my secret never coming out.

But what about Dora? She would be going away in a very few days' time, and could I let her go without speaking to her the words of love which were shrieking for utterance in my heart?

I knew that I could not, try how I would. In spite of the realisation that I ought not to propose to her until after I had rid myself finally of the living-dead woman upstairs—nay, until I had the certainty that I had done so with impunity from any legal consequences—I felt it was imperative for my sanity—imperative, even, for my courage to destroy that which stood between us—that I should have held Dora in my arms, felt her kisses upon my starving lips, and heard her promise to be my wife before she left "Restormal."

But ought I not to confide to her the terrible secret I would carry in my bosom for the rest of my life? The last thing I desired was that there should be any locked doors between us.

But of what use to inflict upon her such a tale of horror which could only make her think me insane? She knew already that I was a widower, and that my first marriage was a miserable farce. Better forget—say nothing—let the past bury its own dead.

Things now began to move rapidly towards the terrible climax. I proposed to Dora in the garden on a beautiful moonlight evening, was accepted, and we were returning together to the house, when, to my horror, Dora, looking up at the laboratory window, saw Mabel's face glaring down upon us.

Poor child, how frightened she was, and it gave me, too, a dreadful shock.

When I had locked Mabel in the attic—which was a windowless room with a skylight—I had imagined that the garden was safe from her observation—forgetting that there was an inter-communication door between the two rooms and that I had left it unbolted.

Mabel had seen my love-making—I could not doubt it, and was beyond doubt gnashing her hideous teeth in savage jealousy. Thank Heaven the laboratory door itself, as well as the main entrance to the attic, was securely locked. Otherwise—

The mere thought was unbearable.

When Dora told me of what she had seen I had to say of course that it was nothing more than a figment of her imagination—and when we got inside the house my mother confirmed my explanation, behaving with wonderful self-control under the circumstances, and getting Dora to bed quickly and tactfully.

Apart from the misfortune of my fiancée having seen Mabel, I knew that this terrible corpse-woman would be beyond control now: that she must be got back to her attic, and kept there at all costs. She must never enter the laboratory again. To see that face in the window a second time would make Dora realise that it could not have been her imagination—as we had now induced her almost to believe—and then . . . horrors!

Thank Heaven I was no longer alone in this matter—that I had an ally in mother.

As soon as everyone had gone to bed, and we had the house to ourselves, my mother and I discussed the position again, and decided that if we found that Mabel had actually seen me with Dora, and was so far beyond control as to draw attention to her presence in the house, the only thing to do would be to make a final end then and there. Together we crept upstairs to the laboratory heavily armed—prepared for anything.

To our surprise, however, Mabel gave not the least trouble. She was in an exceptionally docile mood—and even the presence of my mother (whom she hated with unbelievable violence) did not seem to ruffle her much. So meek and mild and obedient was she, in fact, that I thought that I had been mistaken and that she had not seen Dora and I together that night. After all, it had been very dark in the garden.

Still, I did not altogether trust to appearances, knowing from the experience of many years that she was the most cunning of women, and that this docility might be nothing more than an attempt to deceive. So I got her back into the attic and locked her in, fastening the inter-communication door which led to the laboratory, and locking the laboratory itself.

She was a fast prisoner, and could not even show herself at the window.

After this all went smoothly until late the following night—the fatal night during which matters came to a head—when, after my unlocking the main entrance to the attic to take Mabel her food as usual (I always fed her at night from a morbid fear of questions being asked) I found, upon attempting to re-lock it, that the lock had jammed. Do what I might it would not move.

The door would not fasten, and so, since Mabel could not be locked in the attic, I was compelled to move her for the night into the laboratory.

And this precipitated matters.

Possibly a sub-conscious instinct warned me that I must not sleep that night. Anyhow, I felt very restless and vaguely excited, and so did not even take my clothes off, but sat up fully dressed in my bedroom with a book.

It was well that I did so.

Mabel stole down in the night, and somehow, or other, found Dora's bedroom. She must have had a key to the laboratory door: must have found a duplicate at some time or other and kept it hidden thinking she might want to use it one day—probably to get out and murder *me*.

Anyhow, get out of the laboratory she did—and crept downstairs to Dora's room.

Had I not heard her she would no doubt have murdered Dora while she slept.

Her calmness had been a pose, of course. She *had* seen Dora and me together in the garden, and was at once filled with raging jealousy: jealousy of her own peculiar sort: jealousy born not of outraged love, but of outraged pride and malignant hate. She was far too cunning to show it when I went up to the laboratory, since, had she done so, she knew that she would probably not get the chance she wanted to *kill Dora in cold blood*—doubtless kill me as well: possibly, too, my mother, whom, as I have said before, she hated with a demoniac fury. No doubt she had done something to the attic lock to jam it so that she should have to be removed to the laboratory of which she had a duplicate key.

I arrived on the spot just in time: just at the very moment when Dora uttered a piercing scream. I tore into the room to see Mabel bending over her shrieking victim with upraised knife—another second and my darling would have been stabbed to death.

Hardly knowing what I did, I dragged Mabel forcibly from the room. She was a well-built, heavy, woman, and it wanted no small effort. But I was strong with the strength born of crisis, and forced her, scratching, biting, and struggling, out of the room and onto the landing.

The noise roused my mother, and it is well that it did so, for Mabel, suddenly remembering the dagger, which, strangely enough, was a curio she had taken from the wall of the room in which Dora slept—and whom, no doubt, she had, until she saw this handy weapon, intended to strangle or to smother—stabbed at me with the knife, and, if mother had not seized her arm, I should probably have been killed.

The next thing I knew was that the two women had disappeared scuffling and fighting for possession of the dagger, into my mother's room.

There was a piercing scream, I dashed into the room.

Mother was standing over Mabel who lay prostrate and bleeding across the bed.

She held the dagger in her hand, and, pointing with it to the corpse, said shortly,

"She's dead, Robert. Perhaps it's as well. I have killed her, and not you."

I understood what my mother meant. She meant that, now Mabel had died for the second time, I was a free man. Not

only so but I had been spared the necessity of staining my
own soul with what was tantamount to murder—to say nothing of risking death on the scaffold.

My mother had saved me by taking my burdens upon her
own soul—done my dirty work for me—and saved both my
neck and my conscience.

But how could I allow her to pay for my freedom with her
life, and what peace would there be for me if the thing
should be discovered and she should be hanged?

But how could I prevent it: for the household most certainly must be aroused by the dreadful noise we had made.

At any minute, Mary the cook, Seagar the gardener, my
sister Kathleen, even Dora herself, might break in upon us.

How could I prevent my mother being arrested for murder
when her very hands were red to the wrists with her victim's
blood?

Even if we could palm it off as a suicide, then the first
question to be asked would be,

"Who is the dead woman?"

If I told them the truth they would put me in a madhouse—and what else could I say?

If I took the blame on myself things would not be much
better. I should be hanged, and my death on the scaffold
would react on the two people I loved best in the world—my
mother, and Dora Owen.

Suppose, by some miracle, nobody had heard all that
fighting and scuffling—what then . . .?

There would be one chance of escape to dispose successfully of the body of Mabel. No one would miss her, of
course, so surely it would be an easy matter.

Yes—if the house were empty it would be—but with a
house full of people who might be awake and listening . . .
But what else to do?

We must carry the body up to my laboratory and hide it
there until I could think out some way of disposing of it . . .

Hardly had the thought crossed my mind than my mother
suddenly hissed out in a terrified whisper,

"Hark!"

I listened intently.

From the garden below came the crunch of heavy footsteps approaching the house, and the muffled sound of men's voices.

Someone had called the police.

I looked round that blood-bespattered room in despair. Even if we could just manage to drag that body upstairs there would be no time to clear up the blood. The police, seeing it, would search the house, find Mabel, and it would be all over.

What could I do?

Suddenly an idea—a possible way out—flashed across my mind. It was a forlorn hope enough: a crude, childish, ruse which ten to one would fail utterly. But it was better than to leave things as they stood. It might be just the hair's breadth which made the difference between life and death for my mother.

"Quick, quick," I gasped to mother, "upstairs—into the attic—hide yourself—leave everything else to me."

Like a streak of lightning she flew from the room, her bare feet making no sound, and up the stairs to the attic. I think that she saw how I was going to try to save her. Perhaps we both thought of it at the same instant.

Here is the idea—how far it succeeded you already know. It looks hopeless enough set down in cold blood—but I thought it out in less than ten seconds which was all the time I had to come to a decision—so perhaps it was not so bad after all.

Mabel was almost the living image of my mother save that she was slightly darker skinned—and, since I had restored her to life—very much more wrinkled. But as she lay there covered in blood to the casual observer there was no difference at all—she might well be mistaken for my mother even by a near relative.

My idea was to swear to the police that this dead woman was my mother—let them think that she had committed suicide, or come to any conclusion they pleased since there was nobody in the house who could be reasonably implicated—save, perhaps, myself—and as it was I could hardly be in a greater mess. Mother herself must hide in the attic, and since no member of the household would be missing, why should the police search a lumber room? Besides, even if they suspected that the murderer was an outsider who had somehow got into the house, committed the crime, and then hidden somewhere, and, therefore, they ransacked the place from cellar to garret, they would not find her because that attic had a secret hiding-hole which I had provided so that I could, should the necessity have arisen, have concealed poor Mabel during her second lifetime from a too inquisitive visitor to the top floor. My mother—thank Heaven—knew where this hiding-hole was.

At the first opportunity I could get her out of "Restormal" and, since she had no relatives that she cared about and no friends, there was no reason why she should not remain dead for the rest of her life.

But what about the other members of the household— would they not see the difference between the dead body and mother herself?

They might—if they suspected that they were being deceived. But, as it was, they would put any slight difference they noticed to post-mortem changes in the body. And, besides, my sister, Kathleen, and Mary the Cook, would, both of them, rather die than go near a dead body—that I knew full well.

No doubt Dora would be sufficiently strong-minded to view the body for identification if she should be asked to: but she did not know mother well enough to vouch for her every wrinkle. As to the gardener—it is doubtful if he—a stranger—would notice any difference, and, even if he did,— and I—her son—swore to her—

Stay—there was my father . . . I had forgotten him. He would never make such a mistake. He would know at the first glance that the dead woman was not his wife and the mother of his children.

But, luckily enough, he was away in the Provinces.

He would be sent for at once, of course, by the police.

But then I remembered that my mother and I were the only people who knew where he was. I must pretend that I did not know this—that it was known only by my supposedly dead mother—and thus delay the news reaching him as much as possible.

In the meantime might I not get my mother away from the house, take her to my father, and explain everything?

But suppose he should get the news of my mother's supposed death before I could get into touch with him. It would be a dreadful shock, truly. But it would be better than hearing that she was to be hanged for murder: murder, too, which, to all intents and purposes, she really had committed.

All this had flashed through my mind in an instant, and as soon as mother had had sufficient time to get into the attic, I wiped the handle of the dagger with my handkerchief to remove finger-prints, dipped it in the pool of blood near poor Mabel's throat, and lay it in a position suggesting that it had fallen from her hand.

Then I slipped from the room of death into my own bedroom, where I burned the handkerchief in the grate with the help of a little petrol from my lighter, threw myself on the bed, put the fight out, and lay and listened.

I could hear the police searching the lower rooms of the house, and knew that I had not been an instant too soon—another minute and they would be upstairs—find my supposed mother dead, and then everything would be on the knees of the gods.

It really was remarkable that the roughly devised ruse succeeded as nearly as it did.

As I had feared, of course, I was suspected of having murdered my mother, and arrested. Dora's noble attempt to conceal what she knew, was, of course, quite unavailing, although it showed me how truly she loved me.

I was arrested, of course, largely on account of the police finding that old will of my mother's in Mabel's clothing, and seeing in its provisions a motive for the crime on my part.

Mother had made that will upon my coming of age, and showed it to me in an attempt to dissuade me from marrying

Mabel. Of course it proved ineffective, and, after the marriage was an established fact, and time had healed the estrangement, mother relented and tore it up most likely. No doubt it was never more than a threat. It certainly did not go to her solicitor, and oddly enough, she did not properly revoke it by making another one. She never was a business woman.

Mabel must have wandered about the house at night, found it, and realised that its provisions were directed against her. She loathed my mother, and, no doubt, kept the document with some vague idea of confronting mother with it as a proof that she was "always against her" or "always hated her," etc., etc.—possibly, even, making such an accusation the preliminary to murdering her.

Anyhow, I had not the least idea that the document was in her possession.

Strange how this, no doubt, malicious, hoarding up of that old will by Mabel should—like a legacy of hate—have just turned the tide of my attempt to save my mother.

But for its discovery by the police, I should, most likely, have escaped arrest: and then, I might, possibly, have been able to have got my mother out of the house to some place of safety where she would have been spared an eternity of suspense which culminated in that unspeakably awful tragedy— her finding my father's dead body in my room.

As it was, of course, I could not go to her, and so she must have waited, and waited, and wondered, and wondered, until the strain, the horror, and the uncertainty of everything turned her brain a little. Otherwise she must have realised that I did not come because I could not: that I had been arrested, and made good, or attempted to have made good, her own escape—if only for my sake. As it was, she simply thought I had forgotten her, and so revealed her presence in the house by calling out my name, and knocking at my door.

My confession is finished. Improbable, nay impossible, as it may seem, I declare that it is the truth, the whole truth, and nothing but the truth. Further, I declare, that upon my father's unhappy end I can throw no light whatever, and I look to Detective-Inspector Bradfield to sift this detail of the tragedy to the bottom.

I have nothing more to say, save that I desire the police to lay a copy of this statement before Dora Owen that she may, at this eleventh hour, be fully conversant with the whole of my sad and terrible history, and, thus, may, perhaps, be able to understand how it came about that I withheld it from her for so long. If I have sinned greatly, I have, also, suffered greatly, and that the woman upon the love and understanding of whom *my* every hope is centred, may take the view that to know all is to forgive all, is my one chance of future happiness.

Robert Armstrong

CHAPTER XII

WHEN DETECTIVE-INSPECTOR BRADFIELD had finished reading Robert Armstrong's amazing statement, he immediately formed the impression that its writer was mad, and, accordingly, had him tested by two independent mental specialists without being too circumstantial in the reasons he gave for wanting their reports.

Both medicos reported that, not only was Robert Armstrong perfectly sane, but a man of exceptionally high intellect. When the Inspector received this information he was more than puzzled, and it took more than a whole night's solid thinking for him to come to any conclusion about the business.

At last, however, he made up his mind. First he read carefully the report of the specialist who had conducted the post-mortem examination upon the woman said by Robert to be his former wife Mabel, and which autopsy Bradfield had commissioned in case the dead woman had been killed by some means other than by the knife stab—he always liked to sift everything to the very bottom in such a case. This report stated that the dead woman was about fifty years of age, had unusually withered skin for her comparatively moderate years, and had died from the effects of the wound. There was nothing abnormal whatever.

Next the detective had the grave of Mabel Burne (to give her her maiden name) examined.

It was quite empty in spite of the sworn statements made by the undertakers who had conducted, and the relatives who had attended the funeral—as well as that of the clergyman who had read the service, to the effect that a coffin actually had been buried there.

Not only so, but the body in question, when compared with photographs of Mabel, certainly showed a very startling resemblance. So Bradfield was forced to the conclusion that there was something in this case which was, for once, quite outside his experience.

Finally, he put the case before one of the greatest living authorities on such matters, and asked if it might be possible for a person dead and buried to be restored to life by scientific means.

Here is the reply he received,

"In the present state of our knowledge, it is generally thought to be impossible to restore anyone to life by any means whatsoever. There is no proved instance of such a thing being done in the whole history of medicine. But to say that anything is impossible would require more than human knowledge: to-day's impossibility is to-morrow's commonplace.

"The boundaries between life and death, however, are anything but distinct, and it has been established, over and over again, that people have, when merely in a state of coma, been certified as dead by medical practitioners—and, therefore, buried while still alive.

"Is it not, therefore, reasonable to suppose that this dreadful fate actually befell Robert Armstrong's wife Mabel, and his treatment did no more than wake her from this coma?

"It is said that such a thing actually occurred in London in the year 1831, when a certain Edward Stapleton, after having actually been buried two whole days was removed from his grave by body-snatchers, and experimented upon by medical students. One of them, it is alleged, with a craze for electricity—then in its infancy—connected a battery to one of the muscles, and after the current has passed, the body rose from the dissecting table, and, after further treatment, recovered completely from the coma which had been mistaken for death.

"Nevertheless, we have no actual proof that Robert Armstrong did not, for the first time in history, restore a genuinely dead person to life, even though, when one weighs the probabilities in the scale of what research has, up to now, revealed, the odds are against him."

As Robert Armstrong had requested, Bradfield put the statement which occupies the two preceding chapters of this narrative, before Dora Owen, adding what his enquiries had since brought to light.

She read it through, very carefully and thoughtfully, and then quietly gave it him back, saying,

"Poor boy—how he must have suffered."

And so it came to pass that Robert Armstrong found Dora waiting for him under that same rose-grown arch beneath which he had first held her to his heart: waiting for him with open arms—the veritable realisation of his dreams.

Bradfield was a cynic. "Ah!" thought he, when he heard that the lovers were shortly to be united, "no wonder the girl sticks like glue . . . twenty-five thousand from his mother, and all his father's money as well . . . freehold mansion full of genuine antiques . . . and then his own two hundred a year on top . . . she'd be a born fool to let all that slip!"

And then came the big surprise which, incidentally, cleared up the mystery of James Armstrong's suicide.

Miniature legions of the dead man's creditors swooped down upon Robert as the executor of his father's estate, and it appeared, after enquiries had been made, that James Armstrong had died quite penniless.

Further investigation brought to light that the unfortunate man had, shortly before his end, lost, in one fell stroke, not only every cent of his own very considerable fortune but his wife's money as well, in an attempt to double it on the stock exchange, his idea in taking this risk being to find sufficient capital for an electric power supply scheme which he had long cherished in his mind.

Carefully keeping all knowledge of the disaster from his wife and from his son, the ruined man had mortgaged his house and furniture to find sufficient money to meet his immediate needs—most of which was spent when he died, there being hardly enough over to clear the funeral expenses.

His visit to Birmingham was, no doubt, dictated by some hope or other that there he might either raise more money or, possibly, find an appointment. But this particular point was never made clear. Whatever it was, it must have failed—since Mr. Armstrong, as we know already, put an end to his life in his hotel bedroom on the very night of the murder at "Restormal."

So all Dora got with Robert Armstrong was his own bare two hundred a year. And, funnily enough, in spite of Bradfield's implication, it did not make her love him any the less. As to Robert, well, what did he care about money or property, anyhow? Dora was all he ever wanted.

Dispensing with the convention of a period of mourning for the dead, who, could they have been consulted, would never have desired the young people to delay their happiness for one moment, Dora and Robert were married just as soon as a license could be purchased, and settled down at once, many, many, miles away from "Restormal" and all its gloomy associations, to a lifelong honeymoon in a cheerful little house with a garden full of fruit and flowers, and with one or other of its rooms always flooded with sunlight, complete, in due course, with suitably filled cot. Robert Armstrong, thus having started a new life in more ways than one, did his best to forget the whole of his tragic past, electrochemistry, biology, and every other ology, settling down to that undistinguished, harmless, humdrum, happy existence which, if it is apt to be a trifle monotonous at times, is, all said and done, the best in the world.

Let he who will follow colossal ambition, or seek for great learning, eminence, or power. Even when attained, they are, at the best, lonely, tottering thrones of discontent, while to be a genius, or to be compelled by fate to do extraordinary things for ultimate celebrity at the cost of the power to do commonplace ones to get an ordinary living, is the most miserable fate which can befall a human being. It is better—infinitely better—to be the simpleton who thinks he knows everything, than the savant who has proved that he knows nothing: who, Faust-like, disgusted at the depth of human

ignorance and human depravity, which his long life of learning has revealed, and sickened by his own hopeless attempts
to do the impossible, may summon the powers of hell to aid
him at the cost of his own soul.

RAMBLE HOUSE's

HARRY STEPHEN KEELER WEBWORK MYSTERIES

(RH) indicates the title is available ONLY in the RAMBLE HOUSE edition

The Ace of Spades Murder
The Affair of the Bottled Deuce (RH)
The Amazing Web
The Barking Clock
Behind That Mask
The Book with the Orange Leaves
The Bottle with the Green Wax Seal
The Box from Japan
The Case of the Canny Killer
The Case of the Crazy Corpse (RH)
The Case of the Flying Hands (RH)
The Case of the Ivory Arrow
The Case of the Jeweled Ragpicker
The Case of the Lavender Gripsack
The Case of the Mysterious Moll
The Case of the 16 Beans
The Case of the Transparent Nude (RH)
The Case of the Transposed Legs
The Case of the Two-Headed Idiot (RH)
The Case of the Two Strange Ladies
The Circus Stealers (RH)
Cleopatra's Tears
A Copy of Beowulf (RH)
The Crimson Cube (RH)
The Face of the Man From Saturn
Find the Clock
The Five Silver Buddhas
The 4th King
The Gallows Waits, My Lord! (RH)
The Green Jade Hand
Finger! Finger!
Hangman's Nights (RH)
I, Chameleon (RH)
I Killed Lincoln at 10:13! (RH)
The Iron Ring
The Man Who Changed His Skin (RH)
The Man with the Crimson Box
The Man with the Magic Eardrums
The Man with the Wooden Spectacles
The Marceau Case
The Matilda Hunter Murder
The Monocled Monster

The Murder of London Lew
The Murdered Mathematician
The Mysterious Card (RH)
The Mysterious Ivory Ball of Wong Shing Li (RH)
The Mystery of the Fiddling Cracksman
The Peacock Fan
The Photo of Lady X (RH)
The Portrait of Jirjohn Cobb
Report on Vanessa Hewstone (RH)
Riddle of the Travelling Skull
Riddle of the Wooden Parrakeet (RH)
The Scarlet Mummy (RH)
The Search for X-Y-Z
The Sharkskin Book
Sing Sing Nights
The Six From Nowhere (RH)
The Skull of the Waltzing Clown
The Spectacles of Mr. Cagliostro
Stand By—London Calling!
The Steeltown Strangler
The Stolen Gravestone (RH)
Strange Journey (RH)
The Strange Will
The Straw Hat Murders (RH)
The Street of 1000 Eyes (RH)
Thieves' Nights
Three Novellos (RH)
The Tiger Snake
The Trap (RH)
Vagabond Nights (Defrauded Yeggman)
Vagabond Nights 2 (10 Hours)
The Vanishing Gold Truck
The Voice of the Seven Sparrows
The Washington Square Enigma
When Thief Meets Thief
The White Circle (RH)
The Wonderful Scheme of Mr. Christopher Thorne
X. Jones—of Scotland Yard
Y. Cheung, Business Detective

Keeler Related Works

A To Izzard: A Harry Stephen Keeler Companion by Fender Tucker — Articles and stories about Harry, by Harry, and in his style. Included is a compleat bibliography.

Wild About Harry: Reviews of Keeler Novels — Edited by Richard Polt & Fender Tucker — 22 reviews of works by Harry Stephen Keeler from *Keeler News*. A perfect introduction to the author.

The Keeler Keyhole Collection: Annotated newsletter rants from Harry Stephen Keeler, edited by Francis M. Nevins. Over 400 pages of incredibly personal Keeleriana.

Fakealoo — Pastiches of the style of Harry Stephen Keeler by selected demented members of the HSK Society. Updated every year with the new winner.

Strands of the Web: Short Stories of Harry Stephen Keeler — 29 stories, just about all that Keeler wrote, are edited and introduced by Fred Cleaver.

RAMBLE HOUSE's LOON SANCTUARY

A Clear Path to Cross — Sharon Knowles short mystery stories by Ed Lynskey.

A Jimmy Starr Omnibus — Three 40s novels by Jimmy Starr.

A Roland Daniel Double: The Signal and The Return of Wu Fang — Classic thrillers from the 30s.

A Shot Rang Out — Three decades of reviews and articles by today's Anthony Boucher, Jon Breen. An essential book for any mystery lover's library.

A Smell of Smoke — A 1951 English countryside thriller by Miles Burton.

A Snark Selection — Lewis Carroll's *The Hunting of the Snark* with two Snarkian chapters by Harry Stephen Keeler — Illustrated by Gavin L. O'Keefe.

A Young Man's Heart — A forgotten early classic by Cornell Woolrich.

Alexander Laing Novels — *The Motives of Nicholas Holtz* and *Dr. Scarlett*, stories of medical mayhem and intrigue from the 30s.

An Angel in the Street — Modern hardboiled noir by Peter Genovese.

Automaton — Brilliant treatise on robotics: 1928-style! By H. Stafford Hatfield.

Beast or Man? — A 1930 novel of racism and horror by Sean M'Guire. Introduced by John Pelan.

Black Hogan Strikes Again — Australia's Peter Renwick pens a tale of the 30s outback.

Black River Falls — Suspense from the master, Ed Gorman.

Blondy's Boy Friend — A snappy 1930 story by Philip Wylie, writing as Leatrice Homesley.

Blood in a Snap — The *Finnegan's Wake* of the 21st century, by Jim Weiler.

Blood Moon — The first of the Robert Payne series by Ed Gorman.

Chelsea Quinn Yarbro Novels featuring Charlie Moon — *Ogilvie, Tallant and Moon, Music When the Sweet Voice Dies, Poisonous Fruit* and *Dead Mice*. An Ojibwa detective in SF.

Cornucopia of Crime — Francis M. Nevins assembled this huge collection of his writings about crime literature and the people who write it. Essential for any serious mystery library.

Crimson Clown Novels — By Johnston McCulley, author of the Zorro novels, *The Crimson Clown* and *The Crimson Clown Again*.

Dago Red — 22 tales of dark suspense by Bill Pronzini.

David Hume Novels — *Corpses Never Argue, Cemetery First Stop, Make Way for the Mourners, Eternity Here I Come*. 1930s British hardboiled fiction with an attitude.

Dead Man Talks Too Much — Hollywood boozer by Weed Dickenson.

Death Leaves No Card — One of the most unusual murdered-in-the-tub mysteries you'll ever read. By Miles Burton.

Death March of the Dancing Dolls and Other Stories — Volume Three in the Day Keene in the Detective Pulps series. Introduced by Bill Crider.

Deep Space and other Stories — A collection of SF gems by Richard A. Lupoff.

Detective Duff Unravels It — Episodic mysteries by Harvey O'Higgins.

Dime Novels: Ramble House's 10-Cent Books — *Knife in the Dark* by Robert Leslie Bellem, *Hot Lead* and *Song of Death* by Ed Earl Repp, *A Hashish House in New York* by H.H. Kane, and five more.

Don Diablo: Book of a Lost Film — Two-volume treatment of a western by Paul Landres, with diagrams. Intro by Francis M. Nevins.

Dope and Swastikas — Two strange novels from 1922 by Edmund Snell

Dope Tales #1 — Two dope-riddled classics; *Dope Runners* by Gerald Grantham and *Death Takes the Joystick* by Phillip Condé.

Dope Tales #2 — Two more narco-classics; *The Invisible Hand* by Rex Dark and *The Smokers of Hashish* by Norman Berrow.

Dope Tales #3 — Two enchanting novels of opium by the master, Sax Rohmer. *Dope* and *The Yellow Claw*.

Double Hot — Two 60s softcore sex novels by Morris Hershman.

Dr. Odin — Douglas Newton's 1933 racial potboiler comes back to life.

Evidence in Blue — 1938 mystery by E. Charles Vivian.

Fatal Accident — Murder by automobile, a 1936 mystery by Cecil M. Wills.

Finger-prints Never Lie — A 1939 classic detective novel by John G. Brandon.

Freaks and Fantasies — Eerie tales by Tod Robbins, collaborator of Tod Browning on the film FREAKS.

Gadsby — A lipogram (a novel without the letter E). Ernest Vincent Wright's last work, published in 1939 right before his death.

Gelett Burgess Novels — *The Master of Mysteries, The White Cat, Two O'Clock Courage, Ladies in Boxes, Find the Woman, The Heart Line, The Picaroons* and *Lady Mechante.* All are introduced by Richard A. Lupoff who is singlehandedly bringing Burgess back to life.

Geronimo — S. M. Barrett's 1905 autobiography of a noble American.

Hake Talbot Novels — *Rim of the Pit, The Hangman's Handyman.* Classic locked room mysteries, with mapback covers by Gavin O'Keefe.

Hollywood Dreams — A novel of Tinsel Town and the Depression by Richard O'Brien.

I Stole $16,000,000 — A true story by cracksman Herbert E. Wilson.

Inclination to Murder — 1966 thriller by New Zealand's Harriet Hunter.

Invaders from the Dark — Classic werewolf tale from Greye La Spina.

J. Poindexter, Colored — Classic satirical black novel by Irvin S. Cobb.

Jack Mann Novels — Strange murder in the English countryside. *Gees' First Case, Nightmare Farm, Grey Shapes, The Ninth Life, The Glass Too Many.*

Jake Hardy — A lusty western tale from Wesley Tallant.

Jim Harmon Double Novels — *Vixen Hollow/Celluloid Scandal, The Man Who Made Maniacs/Silent Siren, Ape Rape/Wanton Witch, Sex Burns Like Fire/Twist Session, Sudden Lust/Passion Strip, Sin Unlimited/Harlot Master, Twilight Girls/Sex Institution.* Written in the early 60s and never reprinted until now.

Joel Townsley Rogers Novels and Short Stories — By the author of *The Red Right Hand: Once In a Red Moon, Lady With the Dice, The Stopped Clock, Never Leave My Bed.* Also two short story collections: *Night of Horror* and *Killing Time.*

Joseph Shallit Novels — *The Case of the Billion Dollar Body, Lady Don't Die on My Doorstep, Kiss the Killer, Yell Bloody Murder, Take Your Last Look.* One of America's best 50's authors and a favorite of author Bill Pronzini.

Keller Memento — 45 short stories of the amazing and weird by Dr. David Keller.

Killer's Caress — Cary Moran's 1936 hardboiled thriller.

League of the Grateful Dead and Other Stories — Volume One in the Day Keene in the Detective Pulps series. In the introduction John Pelan outlines his plans for republishing all of Day Keene's short stories from the pulps.

Man Out of Hell and Other Stories — Volume II of the John H. Knox weird pulps collection.

Marblehead: A Novel of H.P. Lovecraft — A long-lost masterpiece from Richard A. Lupoff. This is the "director's cut", the long version that has never been published before.

Master of Souls — Mark Hansom's 1937 shocker is introduced by weirdologist John Pelan.

Max Afford Novels — *Owl of Darkness, Death's Mannikins, Blood on His Hands, The Dead Are Blind, The Sheep and the Wolves, Sinners in Paradise* and *Two Locked Room Mysteries and a Ripping Yarn* by one of Australia's finest mystery novelists.

More Secret Adventures of Sherlock Holmes — Gary Lovisi's second collection of tales about the unknown sides of the great detective.

Muddled Mind: Complete Works of Ed Wood, Jr. — David Hayes and Hayden Davis deconstruct the life and works of the mad, but canny, genius.

Murder among the Nudists — A mystery from 1934 by Peter Hunt, featuring a naked Detective-Inspector going undercover in a nudist colony.

Murder in Black and White — 1931 classic tennis whodunit by Evelyn Elder.

Murder in Shawnee — Two novels of the Alleghenies by John Douglas: *Shawnee Alley Fire* and *Haunts.*

Murder in Silk — A 1937 Yellow Peril novel of the silk trade by Ralph Trevor.

My Deadly Angel — 1955 Cold War drama by John Chelton.

My First Time: The One Experience You Never Forget — Michael Birchwood — 64 true first-person narratives of how they lost it.

Mysterious Martin, the Master of Murder — Two versions of a strange 1912 novel by Tod Robbins about a man who writes books that can kill.

Norman Berrow Novels — *The Bishop's Sword, Ghost House, Don't Go Out After Dark, Claws of the Cougar, The Smokers of Hashish, The Secret Dancer, Don't Jump Mr. Boland!, The Footprints of Satan, Fingers for Ransom, The Three Tiers of Fantasy, The Spaniard's Thumb, The Eleventh Plague, Words Have Wings, One Thrilling Night, The Lady's in Danger, It Howls at Night, The Terror in the Fog, Oil Under the Window, Murder in the Melody, The Singing Room.* This is the complete Norman Berrow library of classic locked-room mysteries, several of which are masterpieces.

Old Times' Sake — Short stories by James Reasoner from Mike Shayne Magazine.

Perfect .38 — Two early Timothy Dane novels by William Ard. More to come.

Prose Bowl — Futuristic satire of a world where hack writing has replaced football as our national obsession, by Bill Pronzini and Barry N. Malzberg.

Red Light — The history of legal prostitution in Shreveport Louisiana by Eric Brock. Includes wonderful photos of the houses and the ladies.

Researching American-Made Toy Soldiers — A 276-page collection of a lifetime of articles by toy soldier expert Richard O'Brien.

Reunion in Hell — Volume One of the John H. Knox series of weird stories from the pulps. Introduced by horror expert John Pelan.

Ripped from the Headlines! — The Jack the Ripper story as told in the newspaper articles in the *New York* and *London Times.*

Robert Randisi Novels — *No Exit to Brooklyn* and *The Dead of Brooklyn.* The first two Nick Delvecchio novels.

Rough Cut & New, Improved Murder — Ed Gorman's first two novels.

Ruled By Radio — 1925 futuristic novel by Robert L. Hadfield & Frank E. Farncombe.

Rupert Penny Novels — *Policeman's Holiday, Policeman's Evidence, Lucky Policeman, Policeman in Armour, Sealed Room Murder, Sweet Poison, The Talkative Policeman, She had to Have Gas* and *Cut and Run* (by Martin Tanner.) Rupert Penny is the pseudonym of Australian Charles Thornett, a master of the locked room, impossible crime plot.

Sand's Game — Spectacular hard-boiled noir from Ennis Willie, edited by Lynn Myers and Stephen Mertz, with contributions from Max Allan Collins, Bill Crider, Wayne Dundee, Bill Pronzini, Gary Lovisi and James Reasoner.

Satan's Den Exposed — True crime in Truth or Consequences New Mexico — Award-winning journalism by the *Desert Journal.*

Gelett Burgess Novels — *The Master of Mysteries, The White Cat, Two O'Clock Courage, Ladies in Boxes, Find the Woman, The Heart Line, The Picaroons* and *Lady Mechante.* All are edited and introduced by Richard A. Lupoff.

Sam McCain Novels — Ed Gorman's terrific series includes *The Day the Music Died, Wake Up Little Susie* and *Will You Still Love Me Tomorrow?*

Sex Slave — Potboiler of lust in the days of Cleopatra by Dion Leclerq, 1966.

Shadows' Edge — Two early novels by Wade Wright: *Shadows Don't Bleed* and *The Sharp Edge.*

Sideslip — 1968 SF masterpiece by Ted White and Dave Van Arnam.

Slammer Days — Two full-length prison memoirs: *Men into Beasts* (1952) by George Sylvester Viereck and *Home Away From Home* (1962) by Jack Woodford.

Sorcerer's Chessmen — John Pelan introduces this 1939 classic by Mark Hansom.

Star Griffin — Michael Kurland's 1987 masterpiece of SF drollery is back.

Stakeout on Millennium Drive — Award-winning Indianapolis Noir by Ian Woollen.

Strands of the Web: Short Stories of Harry Stephen Keeler — Edited and Introduced by Fred Cleaver.

Suzy — A collection of comic strips by Richard O'Brien and Bob Vojtko from 1970.

Tales of the Macabre and Ordinary — Modern twisted horror by Chris Mikul, author of the *Bizarrism* series.

Tenebrae — Ernest G. Henham's 1898 horror tale brought back.

The Amorous Intrigues & Adventures of Aaron Burr — by Anonymous. Hot historical action about the man who almost became Emperor of Mexico.

The Anthony Boucher Chronicles — edited by Francis M. Nevins. Book reviews by Anthony Boucher written for the *San Francisco Chronicle,* 1942 – 1947. Essential and fascinating reading by the best book reviewer there ever was.

The Best of 10-Story Book — edited by Chris Mikul, over 35 stories from the literary magazine Harry Stephen Keeler edited.

The Black Dark Murders — Vintage 50s college murder yarn by Milt Ozaki, writing as Robert O. Saber.

The Book of Time — The classic novel by H.G. Wells is joined by sequels by Wels himself and three timely stories by Richard A. Lupoff. Lavishly illustrated by Gavin L. O'Keefe.

The Case of the Little Green Men — Mack Reynolds wrote this love song to sci-fi far s back in 1951 and it's now back in print.

The Case of the Withered Hand — 1936 potboiler by John G. Brandon.

The Charlie Chaplin Murder Mystery — A 2004 tribute by film scholar, Wes D. Gehring.

The Chinese Jar Mystery — Murder in the manor by John Stephen Strange, 1934.

The Compleat Calhoon — All of Fender Tucker's works: Includes *Totah Six-Pack, Weed, Women and Song* and *Tales from the Tower*, plus a CD of all of his songs.

The Compleat Ova Hamlet — Parodies of SF authors by Richard A. Lupoff. This is a brand new edition with more stories and more illustrations by Trina Robbins.

The Contested Earth and Other SF Stories — A never-before published space opera and seven short stories by Jim Harmon.

The Crimson Query — A 1929 thriller from Arlton Eadie. A perfect way to get introduced.

The Curse of Cantire — A classic 1939 novel of a family curse by Walter S. Masterman.

The Devil Drives — An odd prison and lost treasure novel from 1932 by Virgil Markham.

The Devil's Mistress — A 1915 Scottish gothic tale by J. W. Brodie-Innes, a member of Aleister Crowley's Golden Dawn.

The Dumpling — Political murder from 1907 by Coulson Kernahan.

The End of It All and Other Stories — Ed Gorman selected his favorite short stories for this huge collection.

The Fangs of Suet Pudding — A 1944 novel of the German invasion by Adams Farr

The Ghost of Gaston Revere — From 1935, a novel of life and beyond by Mark Hansom, introduced by John Pelan.

The Gold Star Line — Seaboard adventure from L.T. Reade and Robert Eustace.

The Golden Dagger — 1951 Scotland Yard yarn by E. R. Punshon.

The Hairbreadth Escapes of Major Mendax — Francis Blake Crofton's 1889 boys' book.

The House of the Vampire — 1907 poetic thriller by George S. Viereck.

The Incredible Adventures of Rowland Hern — Intriguing 1928 impossible crimes by Nicholas Olde.

The Julius Caesar Murder Case — A classic 1935 re-telling of the assassination by Wallace Irwin that's much more fun than the Shakespeare version.

The Koky Comics — A collection of all of the 1978-1981 Sunday and daily comic strips by Richard O'Brien and Mort Gerberg, in two volumes.

The Lady of the Terraces — 1925 missing race adventure by E. Charles Vivian.

The Lord of Terror — 1925 mystery with master-criminal, Fantômas.

The N. R. De Mexico Novels — Robert Bragg, the real N.R. de Mexico, presents *Marijuana Girl, Madman on a Drum, Private Chauffeur* in one volume.

The Night Remembers — A 1991 Jack Walsh mystery from Ed Gorman.

The One After Snelling — Kickass modern noir from Richard O'Brien.

The Organ Reader — A huge compilation of just about everything published in the 1971-1972 radical bay-area newspaper, *THE ORGAN*. A coffee table book that points out the shallowness of the coffee table mindset.

The Poker Club — Three in one! Ed Gorman's ground-breaking novel, the short story it was based upon, and the screenplay of the film made from it.

The Private Journal & Diary of John H. Surratt — The memoirs of the man who conspired to assassinate President Lincoln.

The Secret Adventures of Sherlock Holmes — Three Sherlockian pastiches by the Brooklyn author/publisher, Gary Lovisi.

The Shadow on the House — Mark Hansom's 1934 masterpiece of horror is introduced by John Pelan.

The Sign of the Scorpion — A 1935 Edmund Snell tale of oriental evil.

The Singular Problem of the Stygian House-Boat — Two classic tales by John Kendrick Bangs about the denizens of Hades.

The Smiling Corpse — Philip Wylie and Bernard Bergman's odd 1935 novel.

The Stench of Death: An Odoriferous Omnibus by Jack Moskovitz — Two complete novels and two novellas from 60's sleaze author, Jack Moskovitz.

The Time Armada — Fox B. Holden's 1953 SF gem.

The Tongueless Horror and Other Stories — Volume One of the series of short stories from the weird pulps by Wyatt Blassingame.

The Tracer of Lost Persons — From 1906, an episodic novel that became a hit radio series in the 30s. Introduced by Richard A. Lupoff.

The Trail of the Cloven Hoof — Diabolical horror from 1935 by Arlton Eadie. Introduced by John Pelan.

The Triune Man — Mindscrambling science fiction from Richard A. Lupoff.

The Universal Holmes — Richard A. Lupoff's 2007 collection of five Holmesian pastiches and a recipe for giant rat stew.

The Werewolf vs the Vampire Woman — Hard to believe ultraviolence by either Arthur M. Scarm or Arthur M. Scram.

The Whistling Ancestors — A 1936 classic of weirdness by Richard E. Goddard and introduced by John Pelan.

The White Peril in the Far East — Sidney Lewis Gulick's 1905 indictment of the West and assurance that Japan would never attack the U.S.

The Wizard of Berner's Abbey — A 1935 horror gem written by Mark Hansom and introduced by John Pelan.

Wade Wright Novels — *Echo of Fear, Death At Nostalgia Street, It Leads to Murder* and *Shadows' Edge*, a double book featuring *Shadows Don't Bleed* and *The Sharp Edge*.

Welsh Rarebit Tales — Charming stories from 1902 by Harle Oren Cummins

Through the Looking Glass — Lewis Carroll wrote it; Gavin L. O'Keefe illustrated it.

Time Line — Ramble House artist Gavin O'Keefe selects his most evocative art inspired by the twisted literature he reads and designs.

Tiresias — Psychotic modern horror novel by Jonathan M. Sweet.

Totah Six-Pack — Just Fender Tucker's six tales about Farmington in one sleek volume.

Trail of the Spirit Warrior — Roger Haley's historical saga of life in the Indian Territories.

Ultra-Boiled — 23 gut-wrenching tales by our Man in Brooklyn, Gary Lovisi.

Up Front From Behind — A 2011 satire of Wall Street by James B. Kobak.

Victims & Villains — Intriguing Sherlockiana from Derham Groves.

Walter S. Masterman Novels — *The Green Toad, The Flying Beast, The Yellow Mistletoe, The Wrong Verdict, The Perjured Alibi, The Border Line* and *The Curse of Cantire*. Masterman wrote horror and mystery, some introduced by John Pelan.

We Are the Dead and Other Stories — Volume Two in the Day Keene in the Detective Pulps series, introduced by Ed Gorman. When done, there may be as many as 11 in the series.

West Texas War and Other Western Stories — by Gary Lovisi.

Whip Dodge: Man Hunter — Wesley Tallant's saga of a bounty hunter of the old West.

You'll Die Laughing — Bruce Elliott's 1945 novel of murder at a practical joker's English countryside manor.

RAMBLE HOUSE
Fender Tucker, Prop. Gavin L. O'Keefe, Graphics
www.ramblehouse.com fender@ramblehouse.com
228-826-1783 10329 Sheephead Drive, Vancleave MS 39565

www.ingramcontent.com/pod-product-compliance
Lightning Source LLC
Chambersburg PA
CBHW022328020726
47493CB00021B/1265